THE

KLONE

AND

I

Also by Danielle Steel

* Published outside the UK under the title *Passion's Promise*

THE
KLONE
AND

I

Danielle Steel

CORGI BOOKS

THE KLONE AND I
A CORGI BOOK : 0 552 14637 4

Originally published in Great Britain by Bantam Press,
a division of Transworld Publishers

PRINTING HISTORY
Bantam Press edition published 1998
Corgi edition published 1999

5 7 9 10 8 6

Set in Baskerville by
Phoenix Typesetting, Ilkley, West Yorkshire

Corgi Books are published by Transworld Publishers,
61-63 Uxbridge Road, London W5 5SA,
a division of The Random House Group Ltd,
in Australia by Random House Australia (Pty) Ltd,
20 Alfred Street, Milsons Point, Sydney, NSW 2061, Australia,
in New Zealand by Random House New Zealand Ltd,
18 Poland Road, Glenfield, Auckland 10, New Zealand
and in South Africa by Random House (Pty) Ltd,
Endulini, 5a Jubilee Road, Parktown 2193, South Africa

Reproduced, printed and bound in Germany by
Elsnerdruck, Berlin

To Tom Perkins,
and his many faces,
Dr Jekyll, Mr Hyde,
and Isaac Klone, who,
of them all, gives the best
jewelry . . .
but most of all, to Tom,
for giving me the Klone,
and so many good times.

With all my love,
d.s.

THE

KLONE

AND

I

Chapter One

My first, and thus far only, marriage ended exactly two days before Thanksgiving. I remember the moment perfectly. I was lying on the floor of our bedroom, halfway under the bed, looking for a shoe, with my favorite well-worn flannel nightgown halfway to my neck, when my husband walked in, wearing gray flannel slacks and a blazer. As always, he looked immaculate, and was impeccably dressed. I heard him say something vaguely unintelligible as I found the glasses I'd been looking for, for two years, a fluorescent plastic bracelet I never knew was gone, and a red sneaker that must have belonged to my son, Sam, when he was a toddler. Sam was six by the time I found the lost sneaker. So much for thorough cleaning at our house. Apparently none of the parade of cleaning ladies I had ever looked under the beds.

As I emerged, Roger looked at me, and I politely rearranged the nightgown. He looked embarrassingly formal, as I glanced at him, the top of my hair still sticking up from my foray under the bed.

'What did you say?' I asked with a smile, unaware that one of the blueberries from the muffin I'd eaten an hour before was delicately lodged next to my eyetooth. I only discovered it half an hour later, when my nose was red and I was crying, and happened to see myself in the mirror. But at this point in the saga, I was still smiling, with no inkling of what was to come.

'I asked you to sit down,' he said, eyeing my costume, my hairdo, and my smile, with interest. I have always found it difficult to discuss anything intelligent with a man when he is dressed for Wall Street, and I am wearing one of my well-loved nightgowns. My hair was clean, but I hadn't had time to comb it since the night before, my nails were trimmed and also clean, but I had given up wearing nail polish sometime in college. I thought it made me look more intelligent not to wear it. Besides, it was too much trouble. After all, I was married. At that point, I was still suffering from the delusion that married women don't have to try as hard. Apparently, I was sorely mistaken, as I discovered only moments later.

We sat down across from each other in the two satin-covered chairs at the foot of our bed, as I thought again how stupid it was to have them there. They always looked to me as though we were meant to sit there and negotiate going to bed. But Roger said he liked them that way, apparently they reminded him of his mother. I had never looked past that statement for a deeper meaning, which was, perhaps, part of the problem. Roger talked a lot about his mother.

He looked as though he had something important to say to me, while I carefully buttoned up the nightgown, sorry that I had not yet made it into a sweatshirt and blue jeans, my daily costume much of the time. Sex appeal was not foremost on my mind. Responsibility was, my kids were, being Roger's wife was important to me. Sex was something we still played at, once in a while. And lately it had not been often.

'How are you?' he asked, and I grinned again, somewhat nervously, the mischievous little blueberry undoubtedly still twinkling naughtily at him.

'How am I? Fine, I think. Why? How do I look?' I thought maybe he meant I looked sick or something, but as it so happened, that came later.

I sat, waiting expectantly to hear him tell me he'd gotten a raise, lost his job, or was taking me to Europe, as he sometimes did, when he had time on his hands. Sometimes he just liked to take me on a trip as a surprise, it was usually his way of telling me he'd lost his job. But he didn't have that sheepish look in his eyes. It wasn't his job this time, or a holiday, it was a different kind of surprise.

The nightgown looked a little frail as we sat in the satin chairs, me sliding slowly forward uncomfortably. I had forgotten how slippery they were, since as a rule I never sat there. There were several small tears in the ancient flannel I was wearing, nothing too revealing of course, and since I get cold at night, I was wearing a frayed T-shirt underneath. It was a look that had worked well for me, for thirteen years of marriage with him. Lucky thirteen, or at least it had been till then. And as I sat looking at him, Roger looked as familiar to me as my nightgown. It felt as though I had been married to him forever, and I had, and of course I knew I always would be. I had grown up with him, had known him when we were both kids, and he had been my best friend for years, the only human being I truly trusted in the world. I knew that whatever other failings he had, and there were a few, he would never hurt me. He got cranky now and then, as most men do, he had trouble hanging on to a job, but he had never seriously hurt me, and he was never mean.

Roger had never been a raging success in his career. He had played at advertising when we were first married, had a number of jobs in marketing after that, and invested in a series of less than stellar deals. But I never really cared. He was a nice man, and he was good to me. I wanted to be married to him. And thanks to the grandfather who had set up a trust fund for me before he died, we always had enough money not just to get by, but to live pretty comfortably. Umpa's trust fund had not only provided well for me, but for Roger and the kids, and allowed me to be understanding about the financial mistakes Roger made. Let's face it, and I had years before, when it came to making money, or keeping a job for more than a year or two, Roger did not have whatever it took. But he had other things. He was great with the kids, we liked to watch the same shows on TV, we both loved spending our summers on the Cape, we had an apartment in New York we both loved, he let me pick the movies we went to once a week, no matter how sappy they were, and he had great legs. And when we were sleeping with each other in college, I thought Casanova paled in comparison to him in bed. I lost my virginity to him. We liked the same music, he sang in my ear when we danced. He was a great dancer, a good father, and my best friend. And if he couldn't hold on to a job, so what? Umpa had taken the sting out of that for me. It never occurred to me that I could, or should, have more. Roger was enough for me.

'What's up?' I asked cheerfully, crossing one bare leg over the other. I hadn't shaved my legs in weeks, but it was November after all, and I knew Roger didn't care. I wasn't going to the beach, only talking to Roger, sitting at the foot of our bed on those stupid, slippery satin chairs, waiting to hear the surprise he had for me.

'There's something I want to tell you,' he said, eyeing me cautiously, as though he secretly knew I was wired with an explosive device, and he was waiting for me to blow up in a million pieces. But discounting the stubble on my legs and the blueberry in my teeth, I was relatively harmless, and always had been. I'm pretty even-tempered, a good sport most of the time, and never asked a lot of him. We got along better than most of my friends, or so I thought, and I was grateful for that. I always knew we were in it for the long haul, and figured that fifty years with Roger would not be a bad deal. Certainly not for him. And not even for me.

'What is it?' I asked lovingly, wondering if he had gotten fired after all. If he had, it certainly wasn't anything new to either of us. We'd gotten through that before, though lately he seemed to be getting defensive about it, and I'd noticed that the jobs seemed to be shorter and shorter. He felt he was being picked on by his boss, his talents were never appreciated, and there was 'just no point taking any more crap at work.' I had figured one of those moments was heading our way again, as I'd noticed that he'd been crabbier than usual for the past six months. He was questioning why he should have to work at all, and talking about spending a year in Europe with me and the kids, or trying to write a screenplay or a book. He had never mentioned anything like it before until recently, and I figured he was having a mid-life crisis of some sort, and contemplating trading in the daily grind at an office for 'art' instead. If so, Umpa's trust fund would have to get us through that too. In any case, so as not to embarrass him, I never talked about his frequent failures or countless jobs, or the fact that my dead grandfather had supported our family for years. I wanted to be the perfect wife to him, and even if he wasn't the wizard of Wall Street, he had never promised to be, and I still thought he was a good guy.

'What's up, sweetheart?' I asked, holding a hand out to him. But to his credit, he didn't let me touch him. He was acting as though he were about to go to jail for sexually harassing someone, or exposing himself at one of his clubs, and was embarrassed to tell me. And then it came. Roger's Big Announcement.

'I don't think I love you.' He stared me right in the eye, as though he were looking for an alien in there somewhere, and he was talking to that person, instead of me with my torn nightgown and my stray blueberry.

'What?' The word shot out of me like a rocket.

'I said, I don't love you.' He looked as though he meant it.

'No, you didn't.' I stared back at him, my eyes narrowing. And for no reason in the world, I remember noticing that he was wearing the tie I had given him last Christmas. Why the hell had he put that on just to tell me he didn't love me? 'You said you *think* you don't love me, not "you don't love me." There's a difference.' We always argued about stupid things like that, the small stuff, about who had finished the milk and who had forgotten to turn the lights off. We never argued about the important stuff, like how to bring up the children, or where they went to school. There was nothing to argue about. I took care of all that. He was always too busy playing tennis or golf, or going fishing with friends, or nursing the worst cold in history, to argue with me about the kids. He figured that was my domain. He may have been a great dancer, and a lot of fun at times, but responsibility was not his thing. Roger took care of himself more than he took care of me, but in thirteen years I had somehow managed not to notice that. All I had wanted was to get married at the time, and have kids. Roger had made my dreams come true. And undeniably, we had great kids. But what I'd failed to see until that point, was how little he did for me.

'What happened?' I asked, fighting a rising wave of panic over what he had just said. My husband 'didn't think' he loved me. How did that fit into the scheme of things?

'I don't know,' Roger said, looking uncomfortable. 'I just looked around and realized I don't belong here.' This was a lot worse than getting fired. It sounded like he was going to fire me. And he looked as though he meant it.

'You don't *belong* here? What are you talking about?' I asked, sliding still farther off the satin chair, suddenly feeling unbelievably ugly in my nightgown. Sometime in the last ten years, I should have found the time to buy new ones, I realized. 'You live here. We love each other. We have two children, for chrissake. Roger . . . are you drunk? Are you on drugs?' Then suddenly I wondered. 'Maybe you should be. Prozac. Zoloft. Midol. Something. Are you feeling sick?' I wasn't trying to discredit what he had said, I just didn't understand it. This was the craziest thing he'd come up with yet. More so even than saying he was going to write a book or a screenplay. In thirteen years of marriage, I had never even known him to write a letter.

'I'm fine.' He stared at me blankly, as though he no longer knew me, as though I had already become a stranger to him. I reached out to touch his hand, but he wouldn't let me.

'Steph, I mean it.'

'You can't mean it,' I said, tears leaping to my eyes, and suddenly running down my cheeks faster than I could stop them. Instinctively, I lifted the hem of the nightgown to my face, and saw that it came away black. The mascara I had worn the day before was now smeared all over my face, and my nightgown. A pretty picture. Most convincing. 'We love each other, this is crazy . . .' I wanted to scream at him, 'You can't do this to me, you're my best friend.' But in the blink of an eye, he no longer was. In a matter of moments, he had become a stranger.

'No, it isn't crazy.' His eyes looked empty. He was already gone, and at that precise moment, I knew it. My heart felt as though it had been hit with a battering ram, which had not only shattered it to bits, but driven right through it.

'When did you decide this?'

'Last summer,' he said calmly. 'On the Fourth of July,' he added with absolute precision. What had I done wrong on the Fourth of July? I wasn't sleeping with any of his friends, I hadn't lost any of the children so far. My trust fund hadn't run out, and shouldn't for both our lifetimes. What in hell was his problem? And without Umpa's trust fund and my good nature about the jobs he lost, how did he think he was going to eat?

'Why the Fourth of July?'

'I just knew when I looked at you that it was over,' he said coolly.

'Why? Is there someone else?' I could hardly get the words out and he looked wounded by what I said to him.

'Of course not.' Of course not. My husband of thirteen years tells me he no longer loves me and I'm not supposed to at least suspect a rival with enormous breasts who remembers to shave her legs more often than just at the change of the seasons. Now, don't get me wrong, I'm not entirely disgusting, nor am I covered with fur, nor do I have a mustache. But I will admit to you now, as I look back at that painful time, I had grown a little careless. People did not retch as I walked past them on the street. Men at cocktail parties still found me attractive. But with Roger . . . perhaps . . . I had become a little less than attentive. I wasn't fat or anything. I just didn't dress up much at home, and my costumes in bed were a little odd. So sue me. He did.

'Are you leaving me?' I asked, sounding desperate. I couldn't believe this was happening to me. All my adult and married life I had been supercilious about women who lost their husbands, i.e., those whose husbands divorced them. *That* could never happen to me, nor would it. I was about to discover it could, and had, and was happening at that exact moment, as I slipped almost entirely off the goddam slippery satin chair in my own bedroom, with Roger watching me as though he were a stranger, and I were someone he hadn't been married to for thirteen years. He looked at me like an alien from another planet.

'I think so,' he said in answer to my question about whether he was leaving.

'But *why*?' I was beginning to sob then. I was

convinced he had killed me, or was trying to. I have never been so frightened in my entire life. The status and the man who had been my identity, my security, my life, were about to disappear. And then who would I be? No one.

'I have to leave. I need to. I can't breathe here.' I had never noticed him having any trouble breathing. He breathed fine, from what I could see. In fact he snored like a Zamboni on an ice rink. I kind of liked it. To me, it sounded like a large cat purring. But then again I wasn't the one who was leaving, he was. 'The kids drive me nuts,' he explained. 'It's just too much pressure all the time, too much responsibility . . . too much noise . . . too much everything . . . and when I look at you, I see a stranger.'

'Me?' I asked, with a look of amazement. What stranger would parade around his house with uncombed hair, unshaven legs, and a torn flannel nightgown? Strangers wore micro miniskirts, stiletto heels, and tight sweaters over enormous silicone implants. Apparently, no one had told him.

'We're not strangers after knowing you for nineteen years, Roger, you're my best friend.'

But not any longer. 'When are you leaving?' I managed to choke out the words, while still smearing the watery black mascara all over my nightgown. It wasn't a very pretty picture. *Pathetic* barely began to touch it. *Ugly* would have done it better. *Revolting* would have said it all. I must have looked nothing short of disgusting, and to add to the romance of it all, my nose started running.

'I thought I'd stay through the holidays,' Roger said grandly. It was nice of him, I guess, but it also meant I had approximately one month to either adjust to it, or talk him out of leaving. Maybe a vacation in Mexico . . . Hawaii . . . Tahiti . . . the Galápagos would do it. Someplace warm and sexy. I'm sure at that moment he had absolutely no problem at all imagining me on a beach somewhere, in a T-shirt and a flannel nightgown. 'I'm moving into the guest room.' He looked and sounded as though he meant it. It was my worst nightmare. The impossible had happened. My husband was leaving me, and had just told me he no longer loved me. I managed to throw my arms around his neck then and smear what was left of my mascara all over his immaculate shirt collar. My tears fell unseen on his blazer, and my nose ran on his tie, while ever so cautiously he held me, kind of like a bank teller afraid to get too near the bank robber with sticks of dynamite taped all over his body. The one thing that was obvious was that he didn't want to get near me.

In retrospect, I'm not sure I blame him. Looking back, I also realize how little contact we had had for a long time. We were making love in those days about once every two or three months, sometimes as much as every six months, after I'd complained enough about it, and he felt obliged to. Funny how you overlook things like that, or explain them to yourself. I just thought he was stressed about his job, or the lack of one, depending on his current situation. Or it was because one of the kids was asleep in our bed, or the dog, or something, anything. I guess that wasn't the problem. Maybe I just bored him. But sex was the last thing on my mind as I looked across at him that morning. My life was on a tightrope and teetering badly.

He finally managed to unwind my arms from around his neck, and I retreated to my bathroom, where I sobbed into a towel and then took a good look at myself, and saw not only the hairdo that eight hours on my pillow had achieved, but the remains of the blueberry muffin. Seeing myself just as he had, only made me cry harder. I had no idea what to do to get him back, or worse, if I even could. Looking back, I wonder if I had relied on the trust fund to keep him for me. Maybe I assumed that natural ineptitude would make him dependent on me. But clearly, even that hadn't done the trick. I had thought that sparing him any responsibility, and being a good sport about everything, would make him love me more. Instead, I had the feeling he had come to hate me.

I cried all day, as I recall, and that night he moved into the guest room. He told the kids he had work to do, and like a truck with three flat tires, we lumbered awkwardly through Thanksgiving. My parents were there, and his, and Roger's sister Angela and her kids. Her husband had left her the previous year, for his secretary. I could suddenly see myself in her shoes in the not too distant future. And out of sheer embarrassment I told no one what had happened. Only Roger's sister said that I looked like I was coming down with something. Yeah, the same thing she had when Norman left her. Six months of intense depression. And the only thing that seemed to be saving her was the fact that she was now having an affair with her shrink.

Christmas was beyond belief that year, the stockings were hung by the chimney with care, and I cried every time no one was looking. Worse yet, I still couldn't believe it, and did everything I could to talk Roger out of leaving, except buy new nightgowns. More than ever, I *needed* my old standbys. I wore them with mismatched pairs of Roger's socks now. But Roger was in therapy by then, and more convinced than ever that he was doing the right thing by leaving me. He wasn't even in trouble at work this time, and had stopped talking about writing a novel.

We told the kids on New Year's Day. Sam was six then, and Charlotte was eleven. They cried so unbelievably that I thought I would die watching them. Someone I knew had described that as the worst day of her life, and I readily believed it. After we told them, I threw up and went to bed. Roger called his therapist, and went out to dinner with a friend. I was beginning to hate him. He seemed so healthy. And I felt dead inside. He had killed me, and everything I had once believed in. But the worst part was, instead of hating him, I hated me.

He moved out two weeks later. I will try to spare you the boring details, and hit only the high points. According to him all the silver, china, good furniture, the stereo, the computer, and sports equipment were his, because he had written the checks that paid for them, although my trust fund had supplied his checkbook. I owned all the linens, the furniture we'd both hated from Day One, and everything in the kitchen, broken or not. He had already contacted a lawyer, but I didn't find out until after he moved out that he was suing me for alimony and child support, equal to whatever he thought he'd spend on them whenever he had the kids, right down to the toothpaste they'd use and rented videos. And he had a girl-friend. The day I found that out was the day I knew we were truly finished.

I met her for the first time when I took the kids down to him in the car on Valentine's Day, and she was with him. She was perfect. Beautiful, blond, sexy, her skirt was so short I could see her underwear. She looked about fourteen, and I hoped had an IQ of seven. Roger was wearing a ski parka, jeans, which he had previously refused to wear, and a grin that was so obscene it made me want to hit him. She was gorgeous. And I felt nauseous.

There was no kidding myself after that. I knew damn well why he had left. It wasn't just a matter of proving something to himself, as he had said to me more than once by then, or no longer wanting to depend on me (Was he kidding? Who was going to support him, if not me?), all of which would have seemed almost admirable, if I hadn't looked right into that girl's face and seen the truth. She was beautiful, and I (whatever looks I still had, and I must have still had some) was a mess. The uncombed hair, the haircuts I never got, the makeup I never wore, the high heels I no longer cared about, the comfortable clothes that were so much easier for carpooling the kids (outfits composed of my oldest faded sweatshirts, Roger's discarded tennis shorts, and espadrilles with holes in them), the unshaven legs (thank God I still shaved my underarms, or he'd have left years before), the things we no longer did . . . suddenly, I saw it all, and knew it all. But along with the all-too-clear messages about me, I also knew something else about him. It isn't sexy taking care of a man to the extent that I took care of him. A man who lets you do everything for him because he's too lazy to care for himself, or take care of you, doesn't turn you on after a while. I may have loved Roger, but he probably hadn't revved my motor in years. How could he? I was covering up for him, trying to make him look and feel good in spite of everything he didn't do and wasn't. But what about me? I was beginning to think Umpa may not have done me such a big favor after all. Poor thing, it wasn't his fault, God knows. But I had become some kind of cash cow to Roger, an extension of his own mother, who had taken

care of everything for him before I came along.
And what I could no longer remember was
what he did for me. Take out the garbage, turn
off the lights at night, drive the kids to tennis
when I had something else to do . . . but what
was it that he did for *me*? Damned if I knew.

That was the day I threw out my flannel
nightgowns. All of them. All right, except one.
I saved it in case I got really sick one day, or
someone died, and I knew I'd need it for
comfort. The others went out with the garbage.
The next day, I got my nails done, and got a
haircut. It was the beginning of a long, slow,
painful process, which included shaving my
legs religiously, winter or summer, jogging in
Central Park twice a week, reading the news-
paper thoroughly, not just the headlines,
wearing makeup even when I picked the kids
up at school, reevaluating my hemlines, buying
new underwear, and accepting whatever invi-
tations came my way, and there weren't many.

I went to anything and everything, and
invariably came home profoundly depressed.
There was no male equivalent to Roger's
friend, the person Sam and Charlie now called

Miss Bimbo, whose face, hair, looks, and legs now haunted me. The trouble is, I wanted to look like her, but still *be* me.

The process took me approximately seven months to complete after he left, and by then we were well into the following summer. I was doggedly paying alimony and child support by then, had replaced the silver and china, some of the furniture, and no longer woke up every morning trying to think of ways to get Roger back, or kill him. I had called my old therapist, Dr Steinfeld, and was 'working through' things, like brambles, or the fog in London. I had more or less come to understand why he had left, although I hated Roger for his lack of charity. I had put up with his lack of business acumen, why couldn't he have been more tolerant about the way I looked? I had fallen into disrepair like a sailboat no one loved anymore. I had had barnacles on my bottom, my sails were frayed, and my paint was chipping. But I was still a damn fine boat, and he should have loved me enough to see through it. The blunt truth was, he didn't, probably never had. Except for two wonderful children, it was thirteen years wasted. Gone. Poof. Vanished. Like Roger. He was out of my life completely, except to argue with me about changing my plans and keeping the children every time he wanted to be with Miss Bimbo. Worse yet, it turned out that she not only had great legs, but she had a trust fund bigger than mine, which really said it all to me. Apparently, she *loved* the idea of his not working, and thought he *should* write a screenplay, he was so 'talented,' according to what the kids repeated to me, that she thought he was wasting himself at work. Besides, we both knew he could afford to live handsomely off the alimony I was paying him, for the next five years anyway. That was what the judge awarded him. Five years of a hefty alimony and child support and then he was on his own again. And then what? He'd marry her? Or would he finally try to support himself? Maybe he didn't care anymore. Pride no longer entered into it, but it sure made me look back at where we'd started with a jaundiced eye.

We had moved in with each other after I finished college. I'd been working as a junior editor at a magazine at the time. The job paid peanuts, but I loved it. And Roger had been making as little as I as an account exec at a small advertising agency. We talked about getting married, and knew we would eventually. But Roger kept insisting he didn't want to get married until he could support me, and our kids one day. Six years somehow slipped by, Roger changed jobs four times, and I was still in the same one. And then, when I turned twenty-eight, my grandfather died, and left the trust fund to take care of me. It all fell into place after that, though I'll have to admit, getting married then was my idea. We didn't have to wait anymore. It didn't matter how small our salaries were, though Roger insisted he didn't want to live off me. He wouldn't be, I promised him. We could still support ourselves, and fall back on my new trust fund to help us when we had children. I talked him into it, or at least I thought I did. We got married six months after that, and then I got pregnant, and quit my job. And then the great purge came in advertising, Roger told me everyone was getting fired. And by the time the baby came, I was grateful for Umpa's money. It wasn't Roger's fault he was out of work for nearly a year. He had even offered to drive a cab, but with what I had from Umpa, it seemed stupid. My mother warned me then in ominous undertones that Roger did not appear to be much of a provider, and I loyally defended him, and ignored her.

We bought an apartment on the East Side, Roger finally found a job, and I loved staying home with the baby and being married. This was what life was all about. I loved sitting in the park all afternoon with the baby in the pram, chatting with the other mothers. And I loved the security Umpa gave us. It made it possible for Roger to work at jobs he loved, instead of jobs he hated. It seemed to me like we had a lot of freedom. And that was just what Roger had now. Freedom. From me. From the kids, most of the time. From responsibility, as usual. He had everything he wanted, including Miss Bimbo to tell him how terrific he was, and how persecuted he had been. All he had to do was look at her and he could remember with ease how boring I'd been. And why the hell had he come out of it so lucky? From what I could see, he was starting back at the beginning. A new life. A pretty girl on his arm, her trust fund or mine. I wondered how much difference it made to him, and couldn't help wondering if he'd ever loved me. Maybe I was just convenient. A stroke of luck that came along at the right time and made his life easy. It was impossible to know, in the end, what had been in his heart and mind at the beginning.

At that moment, with those questions rattling around in my head, I became one of the walking wounded. Which prepared me perfectly for dating. A new chapter in my life. A new era. And, I told myself, I was ready.

The divorce was final in September. Roger married Miss Bimbo in November, almost a year to the day after he had told me he didn't love me. I told myself he had done me a favor, though I didn't entirely believe it. I missed my old illusions, the comfort of having a husband, a warm body in my bed to cuddle up to, a person to talk to, someone to watch the children for me when I had a fever. It's funny the things you miss when you no longer have them. I missed a lot of things about him at times, but I lived through it. And Helena, as she was called, was now Mrs Bimbo and had all those things I was missing. The unfortunate thing for her was that she had them with Roger. I had become a lot more honest with myself by then, and knew full well the places where I had closed my eyes, the things I had chosen not to see too clearly or too often. Okay, so he was a good dancer and sang a great tune, but then what? Who was going to take care of her when things got rough? What was going to happen when she found out that Roger could not only not write a screenplay, but not keep a job? Or didn't she care? Maybe to her it made no difference. But whether or not it did to her, and no matter how inadequate he may have been, he had nonetheless been my husband. And now he was hers, and to me, at that exact moment, it looked like I had nothing.

I was forty-one years old, had learned to comb my hair finally, had a therapist who insisted I was sexy, intelligent, and beautiful. I had two kids I loved, and bought fourteen incredibly expensive satin nightgowns. I was ready. For what, I didn't know yet. From what I could see, there was still no one out there, except my friends' husbands, whom I wouldn't have touched with a ten-foot pole, though several of them tried energetically to convince me otherwise, and all of whom were even more boring than Roger. But in case Prince Charming showed up, and wandered into my life one day, I was prepared. My legs were shaved, my nails were done, I'd lost ten pounds. And the kids said my new haircut made me look like Claudia Schiffer. Shows you what loyalty can do to a kid's eyesight. By Christmas, thirteen months after that fateful day when Roger sat in the satin chair at the foot of our bed and let me have it right between the eyes, I had even stopped crying. Even the blueberry muffin was a dim memory by then, and in fact, so was Roger. For all intents and purposes, I had recovered. And then came dating. And a whole new life I was totally unprepared for.

Chapter Two

Dating in this day and age is an interesting phenomenon. Comparing it to olden days, medieval times for instance, it's a lot like jousting. Or going back a little further in history, it's a little bit like being a Christian in the Colosseum. You put on a hell of a good show, but you know that sooner or later, one of the lions is going to eat you.

And there are a lot of them, lions I mean. Some are merely pussycats, others pretend to be. Some of them look fantastic, but auditioning for the Colosseum is a hell of a lot of work, and in the end you still wind up in the same place, with a lion looking you in the face, deciding when he's going to eat you. After six months of dating, I felt like a Hostess Twinkie.

It was a lot like trying out for *A Chorus Line*, and I never seemed to get the steps right, no matter how hard I worked on them in the mirror. I met a seventy-year-old woman who told me about her new boyfriend, and I wondered where she got the energy. I was nearly half her age, and I was exhausted. Let's face it, dating is a killer.

There were fat guys, and bald guys, and old guys, and young guys, and men that my friends insisted I would be crazy about, except that they always seemed to forget to mention 'one little problem,' either incipient alcoholism, or some deep psychosis relating to his mother, father, children, ex-wife, dog, or parakeet, or a minor crisis about his sexuality ever since his uncle assaulted him when he was in high school. There are normal guys out there, I know, but damned if I could find one. Besides which, I was completely out of training. For thirteen years I had been making dinner every night for Roger, watching TV with him, or sleeping, not to mention car pools to baseball. I was entirely unprepared for the New Wave of preparing gourmet microwave cuisine, serving cappuccino made from sixteen kinds of coffee beans from African countries I'd never heard of, and sports I had only seen tackled at the Olympics. It turned out that manicures and a Lady Remington were not enough. I had to be able to ski like Killy, swim the hundred meter, and complete the running long jump. And to tell you the truth, I'm lazy. After a while, it was a lot easier to stay home, watch *I Love Lucy* reruns with the kids, and eat pizza. And as I reevaluated where I'd been, by my second summer of freedom, I decided dating was beyond me. I just couldn't do it.

The kids spent July in the south of France with Roger that year. They chartered a yacht, went to the Hôtel du Cap, and were scheduled to wind up in Paris. From there, Roger was going to put the kids on a plane home, where I would meet them and then spend August with them. I had rented a small beach house for the three of us on Long Island. Umpa's money was not limitless after all. Roger and Helena had rented a small palazzo near Florence. And it had long since become obvious to me that

41

Helena's trust fund, if not her IQ, was a hell of a lot bigger than mine was. I was happy for him, or at least I pretended to be, which made Dr Steinfeld very proud. Okay, so I lied to him. I was still somewhat angry, and a little jealous of Helena's legs and boobs, if not her trust fund.

The month the kids were gone was lonely at first. There was no one to watch *I Love Lucy* reruns with, but fortunately it also gave me an opportunity to abstain from peanut butter and pizza. Sam was eight, and Charlotte had just turned thirteen and we'd been having endless arguments about green nail polish and a nose pierce. To tell you the truth, by the second week of my solitude, I was beginning to enjoy it. And despite the heat, I always like New York in the summer. On weekends, everyone disappears. I go for long walks late at night, and sit for hours in freezing cold air-conditioned movies. It was also hard for me to believe that Roger had been gone for nearly two years. I no longer dreamed about him at night, I no longer ached for him, I no longer remembered quite so precisely what his body looked like. I would never have thought it possible, but I had finally

stopped missing him, and his snoring, and the
good times we hadn't had in ages.

The kids called from time to time, and it
struck me funny when Roger asked me somewhat breathlessly how I did it, how did I put up
with them day and night, and was Charlotte
really serious about the nose ring. For once,
much as I love Charlotte and Sam, I was happy
they were with him . . . and Helena. Let her
share her favorite blouse, her best skirt, and the
'rad' silver bracelet she'll never see again. It will
turn up under her bed in ten years' time, along
with her favorite handbag, and a half-used
bottle of perfume. I always look under my
bed first for anything that's lost now. I figured
I'd let Helena figure that one out for herself.
After all, taking care of his kids is part of loving
Roger. Funnier still that she'd almost had her
tubes tied at twenty-five, after liposuction and
silicone, because she didn't want to ruin her
figure, but decided to take the pill instead,
Charlotte told me. Sam just thinks she's funny.
By the third week, I figured she was going
crazy, and sorry she ever married Roger. And
I was growing nostalgic about green nail

polish, and weakening about the nose ring. Fortunately, Charlotte didn't know that.

The house was awfully quiet without them. But I was still getting pedicures regularly, and wearing bright red nail polish so I could wear high-heeled sandals. I had given up dating a few months back, but not my new image. That summer, I cut my hair short. Helena was still wearing her mane like Farrah Fawcett. So be it. Roger loved it. And everything else about her.

And then, four days before the kids were due to come back, I made a decision. I had nothing else to do, no reason to wait around New York until they got back. It came to me at midnight on the fifth day of an unbelievable heat wave. I had seen every movie in town, all my friends were away, and it suddenly made sense to me to meet them in Paris. I decided to fly over on a special fare, and got a great deal for the trip back. And they made it so easy and so painless, it seemed worth it.

I made a reservation at a funny little hotel on the Left Bank, a place someone had told me about, owned by some fading French movie star who served divine food and catered to interesting and elite clients. I packed my bags before I went to bed, and flew out the next day. I arrived at Charles de Gaulle at midnight their time, on a warm summer night at the end of July, and the moment I arrived, I knew it was magic. It was the most perfect night that had ever been, in the most romantic city on the planet. The only trouble was that I was sharing it with a cabdriver who reeked of sweat, and was happily eating a raw onion. There was a certain Gallic charm to it, as long as I kept the window open. I did, but mostly so I could see the sights as we drove through Paris. The Arc de Triomphe, the Place de la Concorde, Place Vendôme . . . and the Pont Alexandre III as we drove toward the Left Bank, where my hotel was.

I wanted to get out and dance, to stop someone, to talk to somebody, anybody, to be alive again, to share it with someone I cared about. The problem was the only man I'd cared about in twenty years was Roger, and he was still in the south of France with Helena and my children. And what's more, even if he'd been in Paris with me, I wouldn't have given a damn by then. I could no longer remember why I'd ever been in love with the man, and like him, I had finally begun to wonder if we'd ever loved each other. Or maybe I'd just been in love with the illusion of him, and how comfortable it all was, and he was in love with my trust fund. I had accepted that possibility long since, but I was also grateful to him that I no longer had to pay him alimony. That little opportunity for growth on my part had ended when he married Helena. Now all I had to do was pay him child support, enough to support a small orphanage in Biafra. Roger was a sweetheart.

Meanwhile, there I was in Paris, staring at the view, looking up at the Eiffel Tower, and admiring the *bateaux-mouches* on the Seine, all lit up like Christmas. Alone, which was essentially what I had been for the last two years, and possibly thirteen before that. What's more, I had not only lost my illusions, my innocence, my youth, when I lost Roger, I had also lost my flannel nightgowns. I had given up a lot for Roger. I had grown used to my own company, occasional solitude, and the slippery cool feeling of the satin nightgowns that had replaced my flannels. I had brought four of them with me to Paris, a new batch actually, since the first ones I had bought right after he left had already gotten tired.

I paid the cab when I reached the hotel, and carried my own bags inside, and when I saw the lobby, I was not disappointed. It was a little jewel, and the most romantic place I'd ever seen, run by a boy at the desk who looked like a porn star. Very pretty, but half my age, and I realized as he took me to my room, glanced sensually at me, and handed me the key, that he had recently consumed an extraordinary amount of garlic, and deodorant was not something he used often.

The view from my room afforded me a glimpse of the Eiffel Tower, and a corner of the garden of the Rodin Museum, and the room was blissfully quiet. There was no sound anywhere, as I climbed into the canopied bed, and slept like a baby until morning. And then, like a baby, I awoke starving.

Croissants and coffee the color of tar arrived in my room on a tray with beautiful linens and silver, and a single rose in a crystal vase. And I devoured everything but the rose and the linens. I took a bath, and dressed, and then spent the day wandering around Paris. I have never enjoyed a day more, seen as many exquisite sights, or spent quite as much money. I bought everything I loved, or liked, and even a few things I eventually decided I hated. I found a shop that sold extraordinarily beautiful underwear and bought enough of it to become a courtesan in the court of Louis XIV, and when I got back to the hotel I spread it all over the bed, bras and tiny underwear and garter belts I had no use for. I raised an eyebrow as I looked at it, wondering if this was a sign from God. Dating again? Oh God, no, not that . . . not the lions in the Colosseum again. I decided to wear it for myself. Maybe my son Sam would love it. It might teach him something. I could hear him thirty years hence . . . my mother always wore the most beautiful underwear and nightgowns. It would give the women in his life something to live up to, and Charlotte something to sneer at. I wondered if she would still want the nose pierce. All I wanted was to spend the rest of my life in Paris, in the underwear that was lying all over my bed.

The hotel had no room service that week, due to a problem in the kitchen, other than croissants and coffee in the morning, so I decided to wander down the Boulevard Saint-Michel and look for a bistro. I had had lunch at the Deux Magots, alone, listening to the Parisians and watching tourists. I felt incredibly grown up as I left the hotel. *This* was true independence. I had finally made it. Victory. In French underwear. I was wearing the pale blue set I had bought that morning, and stockings with garters. But who would know it? Only the police, if I had an accident, a cheerful prospect . . . Like my thoughts of Sam earlier on, I could just hear the French gendarmes commenting to each other what fabulous underwear the corpse wore. But I managed to stay alive, underwear intact, all the way to the bistro. And then I saw him.

I had just ordered a Pernod, a bitter licorice-flavored drink I'd hated all my life, but ordered because it seemed so French, and a plate of smoked salmon. I wasn't really hungry but thought I should eat something, and I found myself staring at him when the waiter set the Pernod down. I was wearing a black T-shirt and jeans, and an old pair of black loafers. I'd left the high-heeled sandals back at the hotel in my suitcase. I wasn't trying to look sexy here, just enjoy myself until I met the children. I had left Roger a message that morning about where to bring them, so he didn't put them on the plane to New York.

The man I was staring at was tall and slim, with broad shoulders, and eyes that seemed to take everyone in. He was long and lanky, and had a way of sitting there, leaning back in his chair, as though he had a part in a Humphrey Bogart movie. I guessed him to be somewhere in his early or mid-fifties, and for some reason suspected he was either English or German. He had that kind of cool look about him. I knew he wasn't French, and surmised from his somewhat complicated exchange with his waiter that he didn't speak it either. And then I saw him reading the *Herald Tribune.*

I have no idea why, other than sheer loneliness, or boredom, or chemistry perhaps, but

I was fascinated by him. With hordes of Frenchmen wandering nearby, I couldn't take my eyes off him. Something about him mesmerized me. He was handsome, certainly, but only slightly more so than other men I'd seen, but there was an aura of undeniable attraction about him, and worse yet, I suspected that he knew it. Even reading the *Herald Tribune*, he looked sexy.

He was wearing a blue Oxford shirt, no tie, khaki pants, and loafers like mine, and as I watched him sip his wine, I realized he was American. I had come all the way to Paris and was fascinated by some guy who was probably from Dallas or Chicago. Pathetic. Talk about wasting the price of a ticket. And then he turned, and saw me. His eyes met mine, we stared at each other for a brief time, and then he went back to his paper, clearly unaffected by what he'd seen. He was obviously holding out for Brigitte Bardot, or Catherine Deneuve, or some French girl who looked like Helena. What did I expect, I asked myself, for him to knock over his chair, fall at my feet, and beg me to have dinner with him? No, but he could have come over to say hello, or offered me a glass of wine. Not in this lifetime. Men in real life don't do that. They glance at you, look you over a couple of times, and go back to their wives in Greenwich. I had decided by then that he probably lived in Greenwich or on Long Island. He was a stockbroker, or a lawyer . . . or a professor at Harvard. Or another deadbeat like the ten thousand men I'd met in the past two years. Probably an alcoholic. A child molester maybe. Or another giant bore, who wanted to talk about his stock portfolio, or his ex-wife, or the only rock concert he'd been to in his life, when he was in college. Either the Rolling Stones or the Grateful Dead, both of which I hated.

There was no doubt in my mind that he was married. He looked like he'd gone to Yale, or maybe Harvard. He looked like he'd break my heart, or walk out on me one day, like Roger. He was so goddam sexy, just sitting there in his khakis and Oxford shirt, I couldn't stand it. And just looking at him, sitting there, I knew I'd hate him. How many lions does it take to eat a single Christian? The correct answer to that question is: many. Or one great one. I had already been devoured, chewed up, and spit out by experts. Like this one. I could recognize a lion easily by then. In an instant.

Snarling at him inwardly, I ordered dessert, and *café filtre*, knowing I'd be awake all night but in Paris who cared, and then walked past him indifferently after I paid for my dinner. I was going to walk back to the hotel by some indirect route, to breathe in the sounds and smells of Paris and forget him. Our eyes met for a fraction of a second as I walked past, knowing I'd never see him again, and forcing myself not to care. I had been obsessing about him all through dinner, and even I knew, or especially I after the last two years, no man is worth it, no matter how sexy.

I had already convinced myself I'd forgotten him as I looked in shop windows all the way back to the hotel, and then turned the final corner, only to realize that the hero in the blue shirt and khaki pants was just behind me, and closing on me quickly. My heart skipped a beat, and I paused, not sure what to say when he reached me. I was still standing there, trying to think of something clever to say, when he walked right past me. Without a smile, a look, a glance in my direction. He marched right by me into my hotel, and I wondered how he knew I was staying there, or why he cared. He was probably waiting for me in the lobby. Clearly, after two years of readjusting to everything in life from sleepwear to dating, I had lost my perspective.

He was collecting his key from the porno star at the desk when I walked into the lobby. And this time, he turned and smiled at me, and something very primal deep in my soul spoke to me. I was so undone just looking at him, I couldn't even hear what he was saying. If nothing else, he was great to look at. Instinctively, I looked for a wedding ring, but didn't see one. He was probably one of those guys who cheated regularly, and slipped the ring off and left it in his pocket. I could only assume the worst about him. In my opinion, he was much too good-looking to be decent.

'Nice night, isn't it?' he asked pleasantly, as we stood together, waiting for the elevator that looked like a birdcage. I had been walking the two short flights until then, but looking at him, I couldn't this time. My stomach had melted into my shoes somewhere and I could hear myself mumble. I had been right, anyway. The words were American. But I could have figured that much out from the Oxford shirt, the khakis, and the loafers. I didn't need to see his passport.

'It's a lovely city.' Brilliant. High marks for that one. Thank God I went to college, and graduated cum laude.

'Are you here on business?' he asked as the elevator came. My God, a conversation. What happened?

'I'm meeting my children in a couple of days. I'm just killing time, and spending money.' He grinned at that. Great teeth. Great smile. Great body. And I felt about as old, and sophisticated, as Charlotte, with or without the nose pierce.

'It's a great city to do it in,' he said easily, as he followed me into the birdcage. 'Do you come here often?' I pushed two and he pushed nothing. Maybe he was planning to follow me to my room and kill me. Or seduce me. Whatever. But at least I was wearing the pale

blue lace underwear and garters. I knew he'd
be impressed when he saw that.

'About once every ten years,' I said honestly.
'I haven't been here in ages. Do you? . . . Come
here often, I mean . . .' I felt unbelievably
stupid. All I really wanted to do was stare at
him. It was impossible not to think of him with
his clothes off. I wondered what kind of underwear he wore. Probably jockeys. Gray or white.
Calvin Kleins. And knee socks.

As it turned out, his room was next to mine,
and all I could think of was the scene from
Pillow Talk between Doris Day and Rock
Hudson, where they're both in the bathtub,
separately, talking on the phone. If this had
been a movie, he would call me. In real life,
he'd have had me committed for what I was
thinking.

'Good night,' he said pleasantly, and went
inside to call his wife and seven children. Or his
ex-wife, and two girlfriends. Or his boyfriend.
Or any combination of the above.

I stood in my room, staring out the window,
and thinking of him. And since there was still a
faint possibility that he was a normal person,

and not a registered sex offender, he didn't call me. But I saw him again the next morning. We left our rooms at the same time, perfectly synchronized, and rode down in the elevator together. It was raining, a light rain, but I had come prepared, and I was wearing a raincoat and carrying an umbrella. I knew I could hit him with it if he assaulted me, and was fiercely disappointed when he didn't.

Instead, he turned to me in the lobby, as I began struggling with my umbrella. He was wearing a white shirt this time, and he asked me where I was going.

'Out . . .' I said awkwardly, 'shopping . . . maybe the Louvre . . . I don't know . . .'

'I'm going there too . . . to the Louvre, I mean. Care to join me?' But what about his wife and children in Greenwich? That's it? Simple as that? After all those jerks who drank too much, and forced me to use aikido on them on the way home, this incredibly handsome man wanted to go to the Louvre with me? I wanted to ask him where the hell he'd been for the last twenty-one months while I was dating Godzilla and all his brothers and cousins. What took you so long, Bozo? Maybe the time was just right now.

'I'd love it,' I said with a smile.

We chatted easily in the cab. He lived in New York too, about a dozen blocks from where I do. And he spent a lot of time in California. He owned a company in Silicon Valley, special-ized in bionics, some kind of combination of biology and electronics. He explained briefly what the company did, and it sounded like Swahili. Whatever he did, it was something high-tech. And he hadn't gone to Harvard or Yale. He had gone to Princeton. And while he was married, he had lived in San Francisco. He had only moved back to New York two years before, after his divorce, and he had one son at Stanford. His name was Peter Baker. He was fifty-nine, and he had never lived in Greenwich. And my own history was so dull, as I relayed it to him, that I found myself listening to hear him snoring. He managed to stay awake long enough for me to tell him the pertinent details. I left out the scene on the satin chairs, and the fact that Roger had more or less left me for Helena, or maybe just because he didn't love me. I told him about the kids, that I was divorced, and had worked at a magazine as an editor for six years before I got married, but I even managed to make that sound boring. I was surprised he stayed awake till I was through with my story.

I wanted to run through the list for him as quickly as possible. I was a pro at this after nearly two years. Tennis, skiing, yes, rock climbing, no, marathons impossible, can't jog anymore due to bad left knee after minor ski accident the year before, but nothing major, no hang gliding, no small planes, fear of heights, a little sailing, gourmet cuisine C–, new sheets, decent nightgowns, wine, no hard liquor, fatal weakness for chocolate, a little Spanish, rusty high school French sneered at by most waiters. The rest he could see for himself. And perhaps, if pressed, Roger would offer a reference. No serious relationships in two years, God had it been that long, but a lot of incredibly mediocre dates in a lot of very ordinary Italian restaurants, and a few really great French ones. Lonely divorcée seeking . . . what? Seeking what actually? Seeking who? . . .

Man in crisp white shirt and clean khakis, with navy blue blazer over his arm, Ralph Lauren tie in pocket. And what exactly were 'bionics'? I wasn't sure, and I was embarrassed to ask him.

He tried to explain it again on the way to the Ritz for a drink, after the Louvre. It sounded pretty good when he offered. He said he had once stayed there, with 'friends,' but didn't elaborate further. I assumed a torrid affair, which gave me something to think about in the taxi. In spite of a certain openness, there was nonetheless an aura of mystery about him. And something very sexy. Just the way he moved, and talked about things. The questions he didn't ask. The answers he didn't offer. At the Ritz, he ordered a martini, and told them how he liked it. Sapphire gin. Very dry. Straight up. Two olives.

By the time we left the Ritz, it was nine o'clock, and we had been together for ten hours. Not bad for a first date. Or was it? What was it? It was nothing. I was a little drunk on white wine, and he was terrific. We ate oysters at a bistro in Montmartre, and I told him about

Sam and Charlotte, and the nose pierce. I even told him about Roger and the scene on the satin chairs, and his telling me he didn't love me.

Then it was his turn. His wife's name was Jane, and they had parted company after she had a two-year affair with her doctor. They were living together in San Francisco, and Peter didn't look particularly upset when he said it. He said the marriage had been dead for years before that. I couldn't help wondering if that was what Roger had told Helena. Or did he have to tell her anything? I'm sure Helena had never sat around eating oysters with Roger in Paris or anywhere else. They had probably gone to discos, or cheap motels, so they didn't have to talk to each other. Peter also mentioned his son, and that he was crazy about him.

We got back to the hotel just before midnight, and rode up in the elevator in silence. I had no idea what would happen or what I wanted, but he solved the problem for me. He said good night, told me he'd had a great time, and he was leaving in the morning for London. I told him it was wonderful meeting him, and thanked him for dinner. It was an interlude, a moment in a lifetime, and as I closed my door and looked around I told myself that guys in white shirts and khakis were a dime a dozen. But not like this one. For some reason, he seemed unique. And he was. I knew it.

Peter Baker was a rarity, a gift, a unicorn in today's world. He seemed like a normal person. A nice one. I could already feel myself being led into the Colosseum, blue lace underwear and all, although today I had worn the pink ones. I wasn't sure what I expected from him, what I wanted, or what he did. More than likely, nothing. But he'd said he would be back in New York, and would call me. No chance of that, he hadn't asked for my number, and it was unlisted. Besides, I was going to be in the Hamptons with the children. And I had already been in and out of the Colosseum. I had been eaten alive for breakfast, lunch, and dinner. And Roger had gotten the best parts before that. I was no longer sure what was left of me, or if he cared. In fact, I was sure he didn't. I was convinced of it as I undressed, brushed my teeth, and went to bed. It was so warm, I didn't even bother to wear a nightgown, and there was no sound from the next room. Not even snoring. Utter silence, until the next morning, when he called me.

'I called to say good-bye,' he said easily. 'I forgot to ask for your number last night. Would it be all right if I called you?'

No. It would be terrible. I would hate it. I never want to see you again. I like you too much already, and I don't know you. Hearing the lions roar in the background, I gave him my number and then prayed he would never call me. The jerks always call, but never the good ones.

'I'll give you a call when I get back to New York,' he said. 'Have a great time with your kids.'

Have a nice life, I said to myself. And to him I said, have a great time in London. He said he would be working, and would be going back to the States via California. At least he wasn't boring. He was employed. He appeared to be supporting himself. He liked his son. He didn't seem to have a problem with his ex-wife. He had never been in prison or jail, not that he was willing to admit to anyway. He was polite, pleasant, sexy, intelligent, well behaved, handsome beyond belief, and nice, or so he seemed. Obviously a sicko.

Chapter Three

Roger dropped the kids off at my hotel with a look of immense relief the day after Peter Baker left for London. I had been to the Rodin Museum by then, and every boutique on the Left Bank, and bought a lot of clothes I wasn't sure I'd know what to do with. They were sexy and young and tight, and I felt a little hesitant about them, but decided that if they didn't work out, I could always pass them on to Helena, or Charlotte when she grew up.

The children looked great when they arrived. Charlotte was wearing pale pink nail polish, instead of green, and had settled for a second pierce in her ear, which seemed to satisfy her lust for self-mutilation, temporarily at least. Roger looked exhausted. He barely said hello, when he ran out the door, waving vaguely and saying he had to meet Helena. She had stopped to do some shopping at Galliano, and he was going to meet her there. In thirteen years of marriage he had never shopped anywhere with me. Not once. Helena seemed able to elicit things from him I had never dreamed of.

'Dad's weird,' Sam announced, throwing himself into a chair with a Mars bar in one hand. They had paid two dollars for it at the Plaza-Athenée, where Roger and Helena were staying until they left the following morning for Florence.

'No, he's not,' Charlotte editorialized, checking out the new things in my closet. She glanced with interest at the white miniskirt with the see-through blouse with the white denim pockets carefully placed where it counted. 'He's an asshole. You're not going to wear that, are you?' She looked contemptuously at me. Welcome back, Charlotte.

'I might, but you're not, thank you,' I said, happy to see her after her month away. You couldn't even see the double pierce, and the earring she wore in it was tiny. 'You shouldn't say things like that about your father.' I tried to look disapproving, but it's hard to fool her.

'You think he is too. And Helena is still a bimbo. She went topless all over the south of France, and it drove Daddy crazy,' she said, grinning broadly. 'She picked up two guys one day at the pool, and Dad said next year they're going to Alaska.'

'Do we have to go too?' Sam looked worried.

'We'll talk about it later, Sam.' It was one of my stock answers, and seemed to serve the purpose at the time. He finished the chocolate bar, without destroying the furniture, miraculously, and we headed out for the afternoon. I took them to all the places I thought they'd love, and they did. And when we went to the Deux Magots that afternoon, I thought about Peter Baker, and wondered if he'd ever call me. Part of me hoped he wouldn't. Falling for anyone again would be too painful. But another part of me hoped he would call.

'So how about you?' Charlotte asked at that exact moment, as I was remembering how

Peter looked the first time I saw him, reading the *Herald Tribune*. 'Did you meet anyone while we were gone? A handsome Frenchman maybe?' Thirteen-year-old girls have the extrasensory perception of highly sophisticated Martians.

'Why would Mom want to meet a Frenchman?' Sam looked bemused and utterly uninterested as Charlotte prepared to interrogate me, and I looked vague. I could honestly tell her I hadn't. Met a Frenchman, that is. I had met Peter Baker, whoever he was. But I hadn't done anything. I had nothing to confess. He hadn't kissed me. We hadn't had sex. All we had done was spend a day together. I hadn't lost my virginity in Paris.

'Nope,' I answered solemnly. 'I was just waiting for you two,' I said innocently, which was more or less the truth. I hadn't had a single 'date' all month, and no longer cared if I never did again. The charm of being driven home by drunks from dinners I hadn't enjoyed, and then pawed by incoherent near-strangers, some of them married, had worn thin months before. I was just waiting for the kids to grow up, so I could enter a religious order. But then what would I do with my nightgowns? They'd probably be worn out by then, so it wouldn't be an insurmountable problem. Maybe a hair shirt would remind me of my long-lost flannels.

'Sounds pretty boring.' Charlotte summed my life up with her usual precision, and then went on to tell me about all the cute boys she'd met, or wished she had, in the south of France. Sam told me he caught seven fish on the yacht, and Charlotte reminded him it was only four, immediately after which he punched her, but not too hard.

It was good to have them back. It felt comfortable and warm, and reminded me that I didn't need a man. All I needed was a television set, and a charge account at my neighborhood bookstore. And my children. Who needed Peter Baker? As Charlotte would have said, if she'd known about him at that point, he was probably a pervert.

We flew back to New York, where we spent a day doing laundry, and packing again, and then headed for East Hampton. The house I had rented was very small, but adequate for us.

The kids shared a room, I slept alone, and the neighbors assured us their Great Dane loved kids. They forgot to mention that he also loved our front lawn. He used it hourly to leave us unavoidable presents. There was a constant chorus of 'You stepped in it again, Mom,' as we tracked his little gifts all over the house, grateful that we hadn't gone barefoot. But he certainly was friendly, and he loved Sam. We'd been there a week when I found him sleeping in Sam's bed. Sam had hidden him under the covers so I wouldn't find him, and it looked like a man sleeping next to him. After that, the dog sometimes slept in Charlotte's bed, and she slept in my room.

Charlotte was still asleep next to me, in fact, when Peter called on Saturday morning, and I thought it was the refrigerator repairman. The fridge had died the previous afternoon. We'd lost all our frozen pizza by then, the hot dogs had gone bad, and the ice cream had sat melting in the sink. The only thing we had left were forty-two cans of Dr Pepper, sixteen diet 7-Ups, some bread, a head of lettuce, and some lemons. I do a lot of gourmet cooking in the summer.

'How are you?' he asked, and I recognized the voice instantly. I had spoken to him twice the night before, or so I thought, and he promised he'd come by in the morning, but so far he hadn't.

'I'll be a lot better when you get here. We lost three hundred dollars worth of food last night,' I said, crabbing at him. He had a deep, sexy voice, but like those people on sex hot lines, I figured he weighed three hundred pounds and wore pants that slid slowly down and revealed things you never wanted to see on a three-hundred-pound man, particularly one who was sweating and smoked cigars.

'I'm sorry to hear it,' he said sympathetically, referring to the food we'd lost. 'Maybe I should come out and take you to dinner.'

Christ. Not another one. The carpenter who had come to fix the loose front step the second day we were there told me I looked great in a bikini, and then invited himself to dinner. I figured I looked desperate, and told him we were going out. 'No, thanks, just come and fix the fridge. That's all I want. Just get over here, for chrissake, and fix it.'

There was a brief silence. 'I'm not sure I know how,' he said apologetically. 'I can try. I took a couple of engineering courses in college.' Oh, great. A college graduate. A refrigerator repairman who was willing to admit he didn't know what he was doing. At least he was honest.

'Maybe you could buy a book or something. Look, you told me you'd be here yesterday. So are you going to fix it today or not?' Charlotte woke up and left the room while I argued with him.

'I'd rather take you out to dinner, Stephanie. If that's an option.' Persistent little devil. But so was I. It was hot and all the soda was warm, and I didn't find him amusing.

'It isn't an option . . . and I'm not Stephanie to you. Just fix the fridge, dammit.'

'Can't I just buy you a new one?'

'Are you kidding?'

'It might be simpler. I'm a lousy repairman.' He sounded as though he was laughing at me. And I was not amused.

'What are you in real life? A dermatologist? Why are we having this conversation?'

'Because your refrigerator is broken, and I have no idea how to repair it. I'm a high-tech scientist, Stephanie, not a repairman.'

'You're *what*?' And then I knew who it was. This was not the guy from Sparky's Cool World. It was a voice I had heard several weeks before, in Paris. At the Louvre, talking about Corot, and at the Ritz, explaining to the waiter how to make the perfect martini. It was Peter. 'Oh God . . . I'm sorry.' I felt like an utter moron.

'Don't be. I'm coming to the Hamptons for the weekend, and thought you might like to have dinner. I'll bring a new fridge, instead of a bottle of wine. Any particular brand?'

'I thought you were . . .'

'I know. How are the Hamptons, other than your fridge?'

'Very nice. My son has adopted a Great Dane who lives next door. And the house has been fine, except for this little problem with the fridge.'

73

'Can I take you all out to dinner?'

With my kids? It was a nice thought, but I wasn't sure I wanted to share him with Sam and Charlotte. In fact, I was sure I didn't. After a week of talking only to them, cleaning up after the Great Dane, who did the same thing in our house he did on the lawn, I was sure I was ready for an evening of strictly adult conversation. I was more than willing to drop them at the nearest orphanage, forget the fridge, or at the very least call a sitter. I wanted to see him *without* the children.

'I think the kids have plans.' I lied like Pinocchio, but I didn't want to share him. 'Where are you staying?'

'With friends in Quogue. There's a restaurant there I thought you might like. How about if I come by at eight to pick you up?' How about it? Was he kidding? After two years of alternately dating Godzilla's younger brothers and utter solitude watching *M*A*S*H* reruns on TV, which were infinitely better than the dates, a civilized person I'd met in Paris and eaten oysters with in Montmartre wanted to meet me in East Hampton and take me to dinner? He had to be kidding.

I hung up with a broad grin, and Charlotte walked back into the room and stared at me. She had just tracked a neat little path of dog doo straight across my bedroom, but I didn't have the heart to tell her. Besides, I was too happy to care after hearing from Peter. 'Who was that?' she asked suspiciously.

'The refrigerator repairman,' I said, lying wickedly to my own flesh and blood, but it was none of her business.

'No, it wasn't,' she said accusingly. 'He's in the kitchen, working on the fridge. He said we might need a new one.'

'Oh,' I said, feeling stupid, and then she noticed the dog tracks that had followed her in, and groaned. I couldn't help wondering what they were feeding him. Obviously, too much of something. Probably a side of beef every day, given what he was producing. And after she left the room, I called the sitter.

I didn't tell them till six o'clock that I was going out, and they were going out for hamburgers and a movie without me. The refrigerator was working again, temporarily he said, but the Dr Pepper was cold again and everyone was happy. I had even gone to the store to buy them more frozen pizza and Rocky Road ice cream.

'Where are you going?' Sam asked suspiciously. I hadn't gone out since they'd come home, and it was obviously cause for some concern. I might get a life after all, and that could pose a real threat to them. Who would be around to drive them to the 7-Eleven? Or change the channels on the TV, or clean up after the dog? Let's face it, I was useful.

'With whom?' Charlotte asked more precisely.

'A friend,' I said vaguely, popping the top on a diet 7-Up and covering my mouth with it, so they couldn't hear the rest of what I wasn't saying. But children have extraordinarily sensitive hearing. Mine at least. She heard exactly what I said, although I had swallowed most of it along with the soda.

'From *Paris*? Is he French?'

'No, he's American. I met him there.'

'Does he speak English?' Sam asked, looking worried.

'Like a native,' I reassured him. They both frowned in joint disapproval.

'Why don't you stay home with us?' Sam asked sensibly. It sounded fine to him. A little less so to me, considering the alternative, which was exceedingly appealing. In spite of myself, and the fact that I knew better by then, I liked Peter Baker, and also knew I probably shouldn't. He was the enemy, after all, wasn't he? But he didn't look like one. And I had spent a terrific day in Paris with him.

'I can't stay home with you,' I explained to Sam. 'You're going to a movie with your sister.'

'No, I'm not.' Charlotte glared at me, suddenly balking. 'I said I'd meet some friends on the beach at nine o'clock.' I hate thirteen. It leads to fourteen, and fifteen. This was only the beginning.

'Not tonight,' I said firmly. I listened to no further arguments, and disappeared into the bathroom to wash my hair before dinner.

The sitter arrived at seven-fifteen, and, glowering at me, Sam and Charlotte left with her in my car at seven-thirty. They were off to dinner and the latest bit of violence on the screen, something Sam had already seen three times, but Charlotte hadn't seen yet, and didn't want to. I waved happily at them from the porch, praying that the damn dog from next door didn't return to leave one of his little gifts to us on the front steps before Peter got there.

I was wearing a white linen dress when Peter arrived, and turquoise beads, my hair looked reasonable, and the red nail polish on my toes was absolutely perfect. Roger would never have recognized me. I was no longer the poor little drone he had discarded for Helena. Nor was I Helena either. I was me. With a knot in my stomach the size of my head, and no idea what to say to Peter. My palms were damp, and the moment I looked at him, I knew I was in trouble. He was much too handsome, too smart, too sure of himself. He was wearing white jeans, a blue shirt, and his feet were bare in an impeccably shined pair of Gucci loafers.

I stumbled through the appropriate small talk, reminding myself that I wasn't a total loss, and all of my friends' husbands still found me

attractive. That had to mean something. But for
the life of me, in spite of that, I couldn't imagine
what this man saw in me. Besides, he had no
way of knowing that I used to have a predilec-
tion for dilapidated flannel nightgowns. And he
didn't know Roger, so no one could have told
him yet how incredibly boring I could be.
Besides, we had gone to the Louvre together,
and the Ritz for martinis. No one had put a gun
to his head. For whatever reason, he had called
me. And this couldn't even be called a first date
officially. We had already done that, in Paris.
So this one would be easy. Or would it? Who
was I kidding? I would have handled a liver
transplant with greater ease. Nothing about
dating was easy for me.

We had a glass of wine first, and I managed
not to spill it on either him or me. He said he
liked my dress, and that he had always loved
turquoise, particularly on a woman with a
suntan. We talked about his work, and New
York, and people we knew in common in the
Hamptons. It was all very grown up, and by the
time he drove me to dinner, the knot in my
stomach was the size of a large peach, instead

of a grapefruit. Things were improving.

He ordered a martini at the restaurant, and I waited for him to get drunk, and he didn't. I guess he forgot to. He talked about his childhood summers in Maine, and I reminisced about a trip to Italy in my teens, and the first time I fell in love. He talked about his ex-wife, and his son, and I refrained from telling him what a loser Roger was. I didn't want him to think I hated men. I didn't. Only Roger. And that was fairly recent.

We talked about a lot of things, and we laughed a lot. And I kept thinking how different he was from every man I had ever known. He was sensible and warm, and open, and funny. He said he liked kids, and looked as though he might even have meant it. He told me about a sailboat he'd had in San Francisco, and how much he had loved it, and was thinking of buying another. He admitted to a weakness for fast cars, and slow women, and we laughed at each other's stories about dating. Clearly, many of the people he and I had gone out with since our divorces had been related. I even confessed how I felt about Helena, and how just seeing her sometimes hurt my heart and bruised my ego.

'Why?' he asked easily. 'She sounds like an utter fool, nearly as big a fool as your husband for leaving you for a woman like that.' I tried to explain to him that I'd let myself go, that I had let my life revolve around orthodontist appointments and taking the kids to the playground. I failed to tell him, however, that now it revolved around getting manicures and taking the children to McDonald's, and then going home to watch *I Love Lucy*. I figured he expected more than that. A heart surgeon maybe, or a nuclear physicist, something exciting and sexy. But he seemed to be doing fine with the white dress and the turquoise beads. It was midnight before he drove me back, and as we walked into the house, I was less than thrilled to find the kids still awake, watching TV in the living room, with the dog asleep on the couch next to Sam, and the sitter asleep in my bedroom.

'Hi.' Charlotte eyed Peter with suspicion, as I introduced them. Sam just stared at him as though he couldn't believe Peter was actually standing there with me. Come to think of it, I couldn't either. What was this man doing in our living room, chatting with my kids about the show they were watching? He didn't even look frightened by it, or by the black looks Charlotte was giving him, and me, standing just behind him. And then Sam looked over at me with interest.

'You stepped in it again, Mom,' he said casually, and I looked down and noticed the pasty little tracks behind me, and smiled at Peter.

'It's the neighbor's dog,' I explained. 'He rented this house for the same month we did. He's been here since we moved in, and he sleeps with Sam.' I was explaining it as I went to clean up the mess and take my shoes off. I wanted to kill the dog, but didn't want him to think I hated dogs, in case he had one. I didn't want him to hate anything about me. And then I wondered why it mattered. What difference did it make? How many more times would I see him? Maybe never. If Charlotte had her way, and maybe even Sam, surely never. Charlotte's glance at him was colder than the refrigerator that had been fixed that morning.

I offered Peter some wine, but he drank one of the Dr Peppers, and we sat in the kitchen for a while, chatting, while the kids monopolized the living room. And eventually, I went to wake the sitter and pay her. He offered to drive her home, but she had her own car, and after she left, we stood on the porch for a moment, and he asked if I'd like to play tennis the next morning. I explained that I was a mediocre player, which was stretching it. He said he was no Jimmy Connors either, he had an underlying layer of humility, with an overlying layer of healthy self-confidence. He seemed totally at ease in his own skin. But he had good reason to be. He was handsome, intelligent, and charming. And employed, which was refreshing. He said he'd pick me up at ten-thirty.

'Do you want to bring the kids? They can play on another court, or we can play doubles.'

'That would be fun,' I said dubiously. But I had nowhere else to leave them anyway. The sitter I used worked all day. I had to bring them.

He drove away in his silver Jaguar, and I

went back inside to turn off the TV, and tell the kids to go to bed. The dog went straight to Sam's bed, a lot faster than he did. And Charlotte stuck around to express her views on Peter. I could hardly wait to hear them.

'He looks like a dork,' she said with authority, while I was torn between defending him and pretending I didn't care. Either way, I knew I'd be in trouble. If I looked like I cared, it would have piqued her interest. If I didn't, it was open season.

'Why?' I asked casually, taking the turquoise beads off. He didn't look like a dork to me. Far from it.

'He was wearing Guccis.' What was he supposed to wear? Hiking boots, or Nikes? The Guccis had looked fine to me, so had the blue shirt and white jeans. I thought he looked cool, clean, and sexy. That was good enough for me.

'He's a creep, Mom. He's just taking you out to use you.' It was an interesting observation. But he had paid the check, so if he intended to 'use' me, I hadn't noticed. And if he had other means of using me in mind, I wasn't entirely opposed to that prospect.

'He just took me to dinner, Char, he didn't ask for my tax returns. How can you be so cynical at your age?' Had I taught her that? Listening to her made me feel guilty. Maybe I had spoken a little too freely about Roger. But then again, he deserved it. So far, Peter didn't. But this was only the initial skirmish.

'Is he gay?' Sam asked with interest. He had just learned the word, and a rather broad sense of its meaning, and used it at every opportunity, but I assured him I didn't think so.

'He might be,' Charlotte offered helpfully. 'Maybe that's why his wife left him.' It was like listening to my mother.

'How do you know she did?' I asked, clearly on the defensive.

'Did *he* leave *her*?' she asked, looking outraged, the defender of wronged woman-hood, Joan of Arc with a Dr Pepper in lieu of saber.

'I have no idea who left who, and I don't think it's any of our business. And by the way,' I said, feigning an ease I was far from feeling, 'we're playing tennis with him tomorrow.'

'*What?*' Charlotte shrieked at me as I tucked

Sam and the dog in, and she followed me into my bedroom, where I'd almost forgotten she was still sleeping with me. 'I *hate* tennis!'

'You do not. You played all day yesterday.' My point. But only for an instant. She was quicker.

'That was different. That was with kids. Mom, he's ancient, he'll probably have a heart attack and die on the court.' She sounded hopeful.

'I don't think so. He looks like he might last through a couple of sets anyway. We'll go easy on him.'

'I'm not going.' She threw herself on my bed and glared at me, and I thought about strangling her, stopped only by my deep phobia about prison.

'We'll talk about it in the morning,' I said coolly, walked into the bathroom, and closed the door. And as I stood there, I looked in the mirror. What was I doing? Who was this man? And why did I care if my children liked him? Two dates with him, and I was already trying to sell him to Sam and Charlotte. All the danger signs were there. This had all the earmarks of a truly frightening story. Maybe she was right.

Maybe I should cancel in the morning. Besides, if my kids hated him, what point was there pursuing a romance with him anyway? A *what*? I squeezed my eyes shut and splashed cold water on my face to douse what I was thinking. I could already hear the lions in the Colosseum beginning to smack their lips, anticipating me for dinner.

I put a nightgown on, turned off the lights, and went to bed, and Charlotte was waiting for me. She waited until I was lying in bed in the dark, and she sounded like the child in *The Exorcist* when she asked the next question.

'You really like him, don't you?'

'I don't even know him.' I wanted to sound innocent, but even I could hear that I sounded lonely. But the truth was I had been. And she was right. I liked him.

'Then why are you forcing us to play tennis with a stranger?'

'Then don't play with him. Take a book. You can do your summer reading for school.' I knew that would get her, and it did. She harrumphed loudly at me, turned her back, and was asleep in five minutes.

And Peter was on the porch with his tennis racket, in white shorts and a T-shirt, at ten-fifteen the next morning. I pretended to ignore the fact that he had the best legs I'd ever seen. I wished mine were as good as I smiled at him and opened the screen door. Sam was at the kitchen table, eating cornflakes and drinking Dr Pepper. It was a serious addiction.

'Did you sleep well?' Peter asked, smiling at me.

'Like a baby.'

We chatted for a minute, as Sam dropped the cornflakes in the sink and they splashed every-where, and Charlotte appeared in the kitchen, glowering at everyone. But she was carrying her racket.

He had reserved two courts at a club nearby, a very old exclusive one that Roger had always wanted to belong to, but your family had to bequeath you a membership. Roger would have hated Peter. Peter was everything he wasn't.

And as soon as we arrived, Charlotte suggested we play doubles. I knew then that I was in trouble. He thought she was being friendly. And she insisted that I be her partner. Peter teamed up with Sam, who was just learning, and was feeling mildly carsick from the ride over. And then Charlotte went to town on Peter. She creamed him. I have never seen her play so well, or with such energy, or venom. If she'd been training for the Summer Olympics, I'd have been proud of her. As it was, I was surprised that Peter didn't hit her with his racket, or try to kill her. She was without mercy. And when it was all over, she smiled at him.

'She plays very well,' he said charitably afterward, looking unruffled by her performance. I wanted to strangle her again, and was relieved when she saw friends having Cokes at the bar, and asked if she could join them. I told her she could, if she took Sam with her, which she didn't. And then I apologized to Peter for her blood lust on the courts. 'It was fun,' he said, and looked as though he meant it. That was the first time I suspected he was crazy.

'She was trying to prove a point,' I said apologetically, and he laughed.

'She doesn't need to. I'm relatively harmless.

She's a bright girl, and she's probably concerned about who I am, and what I'm doing here. That's pretty normal. I warn you, I'm falling in love with Sam though.' And I loved him for it. I had a moment's fantasy about their being friends, and then instantly repressed it. There was no point getting my hopes up.

We chatted easily for a while, and then had lunch with Sam. Charlotte had lunch with her friends on the terrace, and seemed to have forgotten about Peter. Having disposed of him on the court, she had lost interest in him. There were two fourteen-year-old boys in the group who were far more captivating than he was.

After lunch, Sam swam in the pool, and we sat at the side and watched him. Peter and I talked about a variety of things, and were surprised to discover we shared the same political views, liked the same books, and had the same taste in movies. What else is there? Nothing, really. We both liked hockey too, and were longtime Ranger fans. And had visited and loved all the same places in Europe. He promised to take me sailing. I told him about a show at the Met I was dying to see, and he offered to go with me.

It was a terrific weekend, and so was the next one, and the one after that. Charlotte still thought he was a dork, but there was less energy in her complaining. They saw a lot of the sitter that summer. And he even came out once or twice during the week to spend the night at a hotel and have dinner with me. He definitely didn't fit the profile of the men I'd been dating. He was human.

We had spent some serious time kissing by then, but nothing more, and every night when I came home, Charlotte was diligently waiting up to grill me. I would come in floating on the cloud Peter had left me on, and meet Charlotte's gaze like a splash of icy water.

'So?' it usually began. 'Did he kiss you?'

'Of course not.' I felt like an idiot lying to her, but how do you admit to your thirteen-year-old that you've been making out with a man in a Jaguar? When I was her age, they called it necking. I could have offered a history, of course, traveling through the ages to explain the terminology used for harmless sex acts through the centuries, but I knew her better than that. She wouldn't buy it. Lying to her seemed simpler. Besides, I had somehow kept a firm grip on the belief that, whatever happened, and whatever you did or didn't do, you had to pretend you were still a virgin. I had the same obsession when I was dating in college. Roger always thought it was pretty funny.

But Charlotte just cut right through it. 'You're lying, Mom. I know it.' Yeah, okay, so I am. So now what? There was no certainty at that point that it would ever be more than that, so what point was there to making a confession? He had never asked me to spend the night at the hotel, and I hadn't offered either. And besides, I had to get home to pay the sitter. Her parents would have killed me if I'd kept her out all night, and my children would have killed me. Coming home to Charlotte's inquiries was worse than coming home to my parents when I was in high school.

'I know you're going to do it with him, Mom,' she accused finally, at the end of August, and I was beginning to think she was right. As usual, her extrasensory perception was fully operative. We had gotten a little carried away that night when we left the restaurant, and engaged in some serious groping. But fortunately, we had both come to our senses. Charlotte should have been proud of me, instead of looking so outraged.

'Charlotte,' I said calmly, trying not to remember the feel of his hands slipping slowly under my blouse, and the feelings it had reawoken in me, 'I am not going to *do it* with anyone. Besides, you're not supposed to say things like that, I'm your mother.'

'So? Helena is always walking around naked in front of Daddy, and then they go in the bedroom and lock the door. Just what do you think that means?' Another splash of icy water. I didn't want to hear about what Roger did to Helena.

'That's none of my business, or yours,' I said firmly, but Charlotte was not easily daunted.

'I think you really have the hots for him, Mom.' She grinned evilly, the child from *The Bad Seed* dropped off on my doorstep, as

I glanced back at her in horror.

'Who? Daddy?' I hadn't had the 'hots,' as she put it, for Roger in ages, and the thought of it did not cheer me.

'No, Mom . . . I mean Peter.'

'Oh.' The kid never took her eye off the ball for a minute. 'I just like him, that's all. He's a nice man, and we enjoy spending time with each other.'

'Yeah . . . and the next thing you know, you're going to do it with him.'

'Do what?' Sam interjected as he walked into the room with the dog. The neighbors who owned him must have thought he'd gone to camp for the month, but even when he went back to visit his owners every once in a while, he always faithfully left us little presents. 'Do what?' Sam asked again, helping himself to a Dr Pepper. It was late, but he said he'd had a nightmare. So had I. Mine's name was Charlotte. She would have had a seat of honor at the Spanish Inquisition.

'I told Mom she was going to do it with Peter, if she hasn't already.'

'Do WHAT?' he shouted at his sister in

exasperation, as I tried to get them both to go to bed. It was hopeless.

'Have sex with him,' Charlotte explained to her younger brother, as I pushed the dog through the screen door, hoping he'd be enticed to empty his bladder or worse on the lawn instead of on our rented carpets.

'I'm not having sex with anyone,' I said, cutting her off, 'and you're both going to bed RIGHT NOW!'

'Sure, Mom, get rid of us, so you don't have to tell us what's really happening with Peter.' Charlotte managed to look both insulted and disapproving.

'*Nothing* is happening with Peter, but a lot is going to be happening to you two if you don't get your behinds into bed. Come on, enough now.' She gave me an evil glare and took herself off to bed, as Sam yawned, spilled his Dr Pepper as he set it down, and went to retrieve the dog from the garden. They were both back less than a minute later. He and the dog from hell, who wagged his tail so hard in delight to see me that he swept the remains of the Dr Pepper right off the kitchen counter.

I tucked Sam into bed, and sat down on the couch in the living room with a sigh before I went to my own room, to climb into bed with Charlotte. It was hard to keep up the feeling of romance when I was being tormented by the children. And how was I ever going to explain this to them? It was becoming rapidly obvious to me that there was no way I could introduce him in a major way into my household. We could go out to dinner, or take them out with us occasionally, and he could hang around, certainly. But I couldn't even begin to imagine his ever spending the night with me under the same roof as my children. There was no doubt in my mind that Charlotte at least would call the vice squad. Oh well, I thought wistfully, as I turned off the lights and wandered off to bed . . . maybe someday. After Sam left for college.

And inevitably, Charlotte's predictions proved to be right. Peter suggested he come out for the weekend when he heard that the children were spending Labor Day weekend with their father. I was expecting him to stay at the hotel, as usual, and was startled when he suggested that this time I stay at the hotel with him.

'I . . . uh. I didn't . . . I don't . . . I don't usually . . .' I said smoothly, suddenly mortified despite the inroads we'd made in that direction since the beginning of August. And then I surprised myself, as I reminded myself that I was an adult, and Charlotte would know nothing about it. 'Why don't you stay here?' I asked softly.

'That would be nice.' I could imagine him smiling as he said it. And I was still blushing when I hung up the phone. It was ridiculous to be shy about things like that at my age. Ridiculous maybe, but I felt like a runaway teenager about to get caught by the cops when I watched him drive up the driveway. I was wearing pink jeans and a pink shirt, and a new pair of pink espadrilles. I had thrown out all my old ones. And as I glanced in the mirror, I thought I looked like a giant mass of cotton candy, but Peter didn't seem to mind it.

He kissed me as he came through the front door, and set down his bag. That single act seemed suddenly ominous to me and like a symbol of enormous commitment. What if I chickened out, and didn't want to 'do it'? What if I changed my mind? What if Charlotte and Sam hadn't really left, and were hiding in the closet? But I had seen them drive away only two hours before with Roger. Just enough time to sink into a hot bath, and transform myself from motherhood to sex queen for Peter.

'Hi,' he said, pulling me into his arms and kissing me again, as I wondered if he knew I was nervous. 'I brought some groceries,' he said calmly, and then he looked at me with a question in his eyes. 'Or would you rather go out? I'm actually a pretty fair cook, if you trust me.' That was, in fact, an interesting question, to which I was not yet sure of the answer. Did I trust him? The truth was, I did. But should I? What if he did this all the time? . . . picked people up in small hotels, wined and dined them for a month . . . and then what? What did I think he was going to do to me? What if he really wasn't divorced, or had a thousand girlfriends in New York and California? But as I helped him unpack the groceries and he kissed me again, more passionately this time, I decided it didn't really matter. I was crazy about him. And however evil he might turn out to be in the end, he could be no worse than Roger.

We managed to get the steaks he'd brought into the refrigerator, and the makings of a salad. And he set the bottle of red wine down on the table somewhere behind us, and somehow at that point, I lost track of the groceries, and he began to slowly unwind what I was wearing like so much cotton candy. And seemingly effortlessly, our clothes vanished in a path of pink and white and blue and khaki, and the next thing I knew, we were lying on my bed naked, as the sun went down slowly over the ocean, and I was breathless. I had suddenly never wanted anyone as much as I wanted this man, never trusted anyone as much, had never given myself in quite the way I gave myself to him, not even to Roger . . . I was starving. And what happened after that seemed like a dream afterward when I thought about it. We lay in each other's arms and talked and kissed and whispered and dreamed, and discovered things about each other that I longed to know about him, and he needed to know about me. It was after midnight when we finally thought about dinner.

'Hungry?' he asked in a husky voice as he rolled over, and I touched the satin of his skin. But I could only groan at the question.

'God, Peter . . . not again . . . I couldn't.'

He laughed as he leaned over and kissed me, and whispered, 'I meant dinner.'

'Oh . . .' I felt strangely shy with him, and yet at ease at the same time. It was all so new, and so different than anything I had ever known in my life before. There was something so tender about the way he looked at me, so kind, and yet we were friends even before we were lovers, and I liked that. 'Do you want me to make you something to eat?' I asked, lying back comfortably on the bed we had made ours, sorry that we could not stay there forever, but immensely pleased that Roger had taken the children for the weekend.

'I thought I was going to make you dinner.' He kissed me again then and for a minute I thought it was all going to begin again, but we were both tired and sated and suddenly realized that we were starving.

In the end, we decided to pass on the steaks, and opted for an omelette instead, which Peter cooked to perfection with ham and cheese, and the salad he had brought to make for dinner. He was right. He was a terrific cook, almost as good as he was a lover.

We went for a walk on the beach after that, and then came home with his arm around me, and we fell asleep in each other's arms that night, with all the delicious newness and lack of expertise which comes from not knowing how someone sleeps, or what side they sleep on, if they like to cuddle or be left alone. But Peter made it easy for me. He just pulled me to him, held me close, and a moment later as we drifted off to sleep, I found myself wondering if Charlotte would know, with that hideous extrasensory perception of the thirteen-year-old, that we had 'done it.' My eyes fluttered open as I thought of it, and glanced at Peter, and then I smiled . . . he looked so beautiful as he lay there sleeping beside me. Sorry, Charlotte.

There was more of the same the next day.

We made love again when we woke up, and afterward I made him breakfast. We swam, we talked, we ate, we went for long walks. We spent most of the weekend in bed, and by the end of the weekend, more than I wanted to, or would have dared admit to him, there was a part of me that belonged to him. I was falling in love with him. Correction. Past tense. I had fallen in love with him. It had all been too sweet, too good, too right, too tender. I was a goner.

And when he drove me back into town on Monday night, after I closed the house, he mentioned that he was going to have to spend some time in California in September.

'Do you spend a lot of time there?' I asked casually, wondering if he was telling me this was the end of a brief summer fling, or something I'd have to get used to. I figured I could get used to anything for him. I hadn't felt this way since I was in high school, but hated to have him know it so soon. It was embarrassing to be head over heels for a guy I'd known for less than two months. How could this happen to me? I knew better. I had been married for thirteen years to a man I trusted and loved, and he had still managed to look me in the eye and tell me he didn't love me. This one would too eventually. I knew that. I was a grown-up. So I figured the announcement about California had a deeper meaning. But he seemed relaxed when he said it, and when we stopped outside my building, he kissed me.

'Everything's okay, Steph,' he said, as though he had sensed my panic. 'And don't worry about the trip. I'll only be out there for two weeks this time.' My heart pounded a little. It was as though he understood what I was feeling and the fact that now I would really miss him. 'But I have a surprise for you while I'm gone. You won't even miss me.'

'What is it?' I asked naively, relieved by everything he'd said so far. He was going to California, but he didn't appear to be leaving the relationship. Yet. And I couldn't help wondering what the surprise was. I asked him about it, as he helped me get my bags upstairs. As usual, the doorman vanished as soon as he saw them.

'You'll see,' Peter said mysteriously, referring to the surprise again. 'You won't be lonely for a minute,' he promised. He was leaving in two days, which gave us a little time to enjoy New York together.

The night before he left he took me to dinner at '21' and everyone knew him there. And then we went back to his apartment and made love. It was even better than it had been over the weekend. The time I spent with Peter was magical, and I was sad to remember that he was leaving in the morning. The kids were with Roger and Helena for the night I spent with him, and when he dropped me off at my place in the morning, he told me he loved me, and I told him I loved him too. That was before I knew what the surprise was. I had forgotten about the surprise momentarily. It seemed suddenly unimportant in light of what he had just said. He'd said he loved me. But what did that mean?

Chapter Four

Peter called from the airport before he left, and he sounded in good spirits. He made a vague reference to the surprise again, and then he had to dash to get on the plane, before he missed it.

It was an odd feeling after he left. I had gotten strangely used to him in the short time we'd been together. It had all the elements of a fabulous romance, and yet there was a comfort level, and an ease with each other that was almost like being married. I loved being with him. There had never been anyone like him in my life. Not even Roger. This was very different. It was more grown up, more respectful, more comfortable in many ways. We had a great time, laughed a lot, talked constantly, and enjoyed being together. And there were none of the dead spots, or disappointments there had been with Roger. Peter was terrific.

He had won Sam over weeks before, but Charlotte was continuing to glower. She still attributed the worst motives possible to him, and cast aspersions on him at every opportunity, probably because he liked me, and made me happy. He was aware of her hostility, but didn't seem bothered by it, which made him seem like even more of a hero to me. No matter how much abuse she heaped on him, subtly or otherwise, he was good-natured about it. Nothing seemed to bother him. He was the consummate good sport, and really did seem to like my children.

Later that day Charlotte was in the process of telling me how glad she was that he was gone and that she hoped his plane crashed, as she described the flames that would devour him after it did, when the doorbell rang. I was cooking dinner, and didn't like what she was saying, since I knew he was still en route to California, or at least I thought so. That is, until

I answered the door, wearing an apron, and carrying a ladle. It was the first week of school, and Sam was in his room, doing homework. Charlotte disappeared to hers at the sound of the doorbell, as though she knew what was coming.

I was surprised the doorman hadn't announced who was coming up, and figured whoever it was had slipped past him, or maybe it was someone from the building, with a package for me. But I was in no way prepared for what I saw, when I opened the door, and almost dropped the ladle I was holding. It was Peter, in an outfit the likes of which I had never seen, anywhere, at any time, on anyone, and certainly not on Peter. He was wearing fluorescent green satin pants, skintight and startlingly revealing, with a see-through black net shirt, with a little sparkle to it, and a pair of black satin cowboy boots I'd seen in a Versace ad, with rhinestone buckles. I remember distinctly wondering who on earth would wear them, when I saw it. His hair was slicked back, differently than he normally wore it, and he was smiling at me. It was Peter, there was no doubt about that, and he had played the best joke on me. He hadn't left town at all. He had stayed, and dressed up for Halloween, a little early to be sure. It was a far cry from his immaculate white jeans, and well-pressed khakis, and the blue Oxford shirts I had grown so fond of.

I threw my arms around his neck and laughed. It was a terrific trick to play, and I loved it. 'You're here! . . . And that's quite an outfit!' I noticed that he was wearing a different aftershave. I liked it, but it was a lot stronger, and made me sneeze. And as he followed me back into the kitchen, he walked with an outrageous swagger. He was almost grinding his hips, and in the clothes he was wearing, reminded me of an interesting cross between Liberace, Elvis, and Michael Jackson. He looked as though he were about to go onstage in Las Vegas.

'Do you like it?' He seemed pleased that I liked what he was wearing, and smiled broadly at me.

'It's quite a surprise . . . What I like best is that you're here.' I couldn't stop grinning as I

watched him, and put down the ladle as I stared
at him sauntering around my kitchen. I could
hardly wait till the kids saw him, particularly
Charlotte, who had just been complaining
about how conservative he was, and how
boring. This was definitely not boring, neither
the trick he had played, nor the outfit he had
worn to do it.

'He told you I was coming, didn't he?' he
asked, as he straddled one of my kitchen chairs,
and ran a hand up the skirt I was wearing. It
was a gesture he had never before made with
the kids so near at hand. But fortunately, they
were both in their rooms, doing their homework.

'Who?' I was confused by the question. No
one had spoiled the surprise, how could they?
I hadn't met many of his friends yet. It was still
too soon, and he hadn't had time to introduce
me.

'Peter,' he said, sliding his other hand up the
other leg, as I pulled away gently. If one of the
children walked in, I didn't want them to see
that. It might shock them, but the sensations he
was causing were certainly pleasant.

'Peter who?' He was so distracting, between the way he looked and the way he behaved, and the very fact that he was there, that I couldn't concentrate on what he was saying. I still couldn't get over the fact that he hadn't gone to California, and I was pleased that he hadn't.

He spoke as though to a child, with careful patience, as I gently avoided his hands this time and looked at him, trying to understand what he was saying. 'Didn't Peter tell you I'd be here?'

'Very funny. No, you didn't tell me you'd be here. You told me you were going to San Francisco, and I'm thrilled you didn't.'

'I did,' he said smiling ingenuously. 'I mean, he did. He left this morning. He told me to get here by dinner. He told me you'd be out before that, picking up the children at school.'

'You are utterly outrageous,' I said, laughing openly. 'Are you pretending *not* to be Peter? Is that the game here?' It was very clever, and it totally amused me. He looked so out of character, it was perfect.

'I'm not pretending anything. It has taken

years to perfect me. It was only an experiment at first. But it's been so successful, he wanted to share the secret with you.'

'What secret?' I was amused but baffled. He was talking in riddles. Perhaps it went with the costume, which was a great one. The fluorescent green pants looked like they were going to burst into flames as he moved lithely around my kitchen.

'I'm the secret!' he said proudly. 'Didn't he tell you anything before he left?' He was smiling, and I was too.

'He said I was going to get a surprise,' I said, falling into the game with him, without intending to. It was hard not to.

'*I'm* the surprise,' he said proudly, 'and the secret. They cloned him.'

'Who cloned him? Cloned who? What are you talking about?' I was laughing, but suddenly nervous. This was unnerving. I was beginning to wonder if he had a twin, or a far more unusual sense of humor than I had at first suspected. The fluorescent green pants were the first clue.

'The lab,' he explained, while opening

cupboards and looking for something. 'Peter must have told you he was in bionics. I'm his most successful experiment so far,' he said proudly.

'What are you looking for?' He was pulling everything out, and seemed very determined to find whatever it was he wanted.

'The bourbon,' he said simply.

'You don't drink bourbon,' I reminded him, wondering if that was part of the act too. And then suddenly I had a terrifying insight. What if he was schizophrenic, or had multiple personalities? Was that possible? Could that happen? Maybe as loving and wonderful as he was, he was crazy. Maybe there was no genetic engineering firm in San Francisco. Maybe there had never been a wife, or a son, or any of it. I started to panic as he poured himself a full glass of straight bourbon. This was no longer funny. It was much too convincing. 'What are you doing?' He had filled the glass by then, and all I could think of was Joanne Woodward in the movie about the woman with the dozens of different personalities possessing her. I had seen it as a child and been terrified by it. This was almost as scary. Maybe worse. He seemed to believe what he was saying to me.

'He doesn't drink bourbon,' he explained, sitting down again, but this time the roving hand was holding his glass of bourbon. He didn't even bother to put water, soda, or ice cubes in it, and began guzzling it like Dr Pepper. 'I drink bourbon,' he said happily after the first long swallow. Half the glass was instantly empty. 'He drinks martinis.'

'Peter, stop it. I'm happy you're here. It's a wonderful surprise. But stop playing this game. It's making me nervous.'

'Why?' He looked hurt when I said it, and took another gulp of the bourbon, and then burped loudly and wiped his mouth with his sleeve. 'Don't be nervous, Steph. It's not a game. This is Peter's present to you. He had me sent from California just for you.'

'How did you get here? By UFO, with aliens driving? Peter, stop it!'

'My name's not Peter. It's Paul. Paul Klone.' He stood up and bowed low, sloshing a little of the bourbon on his fluorescent green pants,

but he didn't seem to mind it. I was mesmerized by him.

'Why are you doing this?' I grinned at him.
'Stop teasing me. This is crazy.'

'It's not crazy. It's wonderful,' he said
proudly. 'Ten years ago, no one could have
done this. It's his research that made me
possible, you know. He's a genius.'

'No, he's a nutcase, apparently.' And then I
narrowed my eyes at him, wondering suddenly
if this was his twin, and the surprise was that I'd
never known it. But it was a hell of a way to
introduce me to him. 'Tell me the truth, are you
his brother?'

'No, nothing that mundane. I am truly what
I told you. My name is Paul, and I can do everything he does . . . except,' he looked apologetic,
'wear khakis. I can't stand them. He tried
programming me for that at first, but it kept
screwing up my systems. You know the blazer,
the white shirt, those awful ties he wears. Short-
circuited me completely, so he lets me pick my
own wardrobe.' He pointed to the satin boots
with the rhinestone buckles, and I stared at

them. This was madness in its highest form. After all the wonderful times we'd shared in the past month, this was suddenly a nightmare. This was worse than Roger telling me he didn't love me. Peter was crazy. 'You're the same color as my pants,' he said sympathetically. 'Are you pregnant?'

'I don't think so,' I said wanly, but I was actually dizzy. If it was an act, it was the best one I'd ever seen. If not, if he truly believed what he was saying, he was a very sick man. I had fallen in love with someone so sick, so insane, that it didn't bear thinking.

'Would you like to get pregnant?' he asked me then, pouring himself another full glass of bourbon. He had a mild case of the hiccups, and then suddenly I smelled something burning. It was our dinner. I had a chicken in the oven that looked like it had been incinerated when I opened the oven door to check it. 'Don't worry. I can take you out to dinner. I have his American Express card. He doesn't know.' He looked very pleased about it.

'Peter, I am feeling too ill to go anywhere.

This is *not* funny.' And I meant it. I had had
enough of the game by then. But he was loving
every minute of it.

'I'm sorry.' He looked crestfallen. He could
see now how upset I was, but it only made the
hiccups worse. What were the children going
to think when they saw him, if he kept telling
this insane story? Either he or I belonged in
Bellevue. And I was ready to volunteer if he
didn't start sounding normal again shortly.
'You know, if you want to get pregnant, Steph,
it's probably easier for me than for him. They
worked all the kinks out of that last year.'

'I'm relieved to hear it. And no, I don't want
to get pregnant. I just want you to behave like
the man I fell in love with.' I was about to burst
into tears, but I didn't want to seem like a bad
sport, if he was just kidding. I was praying that
it was just a side of his sense of humor I'd never
seen before, combined with the bourbon. He
poured a third glass then, while I stared at him.

'I'm actually a lot nicer than he is, Steph. To
know me is to love me.' He giggled then and
set down the bourbon, and came over to put his
arms around me. And suddenly everything

about him felt familiar again, despite the after-shave that tickled my nose. I leaned my head against the ridiculous black shirt, and I could see his chest through it. He was wearing a large diamond peace sign on a diamond chain that I hadn't noticed until then. And he saw that I'd seen it. 'Great-looking, isn't it? I had it made by Cartier.'

'I think I'm having a nervous breakdown.' All I wanted was a Valium. I still had some left from the prescription the doctor had given me when Roger left me. But I wasn't sure if I should take it. Five more minutes of this, though, and I knew I'd have to.

'Sweetheart, look at me.' I looked up at him then, and realized that it was over. He was going to be Peter again, and stop playing mind games with me. I was exhausted. The 'surprise' had gotten out of hand, and was now the size of the cloud over Hiroshima. 'I'm here for two weeks, while he's gone. Let's just enjoy it.'

'You're making me crazy.' I was almost in tears by then, and it was going to take more than Valium to restore me. By then my sanity, if not his, was in question.

'I'm going to make you so happy you won't even want him back when he comes back from California.'

'I want him back *now*!' I shouted at him, hoping to frighten away the insane spirit that had possessed him, and was now trying to unhook my bra as he put his arms around me. 'I want you to leave here.'

'I can't,' he said gently, reminding me instantly of Peter's tenderness with me, and I started to cry as I leaned my head against his shoulder. This was insane. I was in love with a complete lunatic. And even this other, utterly crazy, side of him was endearing. 'I promised him I'd take care of you till he got back. I can't leave you. He'd kill me.'

'I'm going to kill you if you don't stop this,' I said wanly.

'Just relax. Come on, I'll help you cook dinner. You just sit down for a minute, and I'll get things organized for you. Here, try this, you'll feel better.' He handed me the glass of bourbon, and put the other apron on. And as I stared at him, he whipped around the kitchen with ease. I felt as though my life had been taken over by Martians. He added half a dozen spices to the soup I'd had on the stove, and put a frozen pizza in the oven, and without saying a word, made a salad and a loaf of garlic bread. And ten minutes later, he turned to me with a smile and announced that dinner was ready. 'Do you want me to call the children?' he asked helpfully. The hiccups were gone by then, and he took another swig of bourbon.

'What am I going to tell them?' I asked, feeling desperate and a little woozy. I'd been drinking his bourbon. I needed it a lot more than he did. 'Are you going to keep this up all the way through dinner?'

'They'll get used to me, Steph. And so will you. I promise. None of you may want him back in two weeks. I'm a lot more fun than he is. And I cook better . . . not to mention . . .' He reached for my bra again and I leaned away from him in terror.

'Please! . . . for God's sake, Peter . . . not now!' What was I saying? Not now. Not ever! Not with this crazy man. Peter had always kept his passion confined to the bedroom. In this new guise, he seemed to have no inhibitions whatsoever.

'I'll call the kids, you just sit there!' he said sweetly, and before I could stop him, he had taken off down the hall to call them. 'Kids! Dinner!' And before I could say anything at all, Sam rushed in and then stopped dead when he saw him, and grinned from ear to ear.

'Wow! Is that how you dress in California?'

'Actually, I got the pants in Milan last summer,' he said proudly. 'Do you like them?'

'Yeah . . . kind of . . . they're rad!' Sam was smiling up at him in amusement. 'I'll bet Mom doesn't though.' He glanced at me to check my reaction, and I was feeling too sick to say anything. I just nodded and smiled, as Charlotte walked into the kitchen and whistled.

'What happened? Did you go down to the Village today, Peter? I thought you were in California. You look like a rock star.'

'Thank you, Charlotte.' He smiled at her, as he put dinner on the table. 'Your mother thought you'd be horrified.'

'No, but I'll bet she was,' she guffawed as she sat down at the table across from me, and I felt as though I had lost control of my life in a matter of moments. 'I bought a shirt like that once. Mom made me take it back. She said I looked like a slut in it.' I took another swig of bourbon while Peter or Paul, or whoever he thought he was, sliced the pizza.

'I'll lend you this one, if your mother lets me,' he said magnanimously, as the children commented on how good the soup was. He had put too much spice in it, but they seemed to love it. And I was always so careful not to. Sam hated spicy things, and Charlotte always complained about my cooking. But they ate everything he'd made, and even had seconds. I was drunk halfway through dinner.

'What's wrong, Mom? You look sick,' Sam commented, between bantering with the madman who had cooked our dinner. The clean, cool, conservative man I had once known as Peter. I was beginning to think he was gone forever. Or I was.

'I'm just tired . . .' I explained vaguely.

'What are you drinking?' Sam asked with interest.

'Tea,' I said, sounding like an alcoholic.

121

'It smells like whiskey,' Charlotte commented as she helped clear the dishes. She never helped me clear unless I threatened her life. All it took was a see-through shirt and a pair of fluorescent green pants to enlist her assistance.

'Your mother's had a hard day,' Peter, alias Paul, explained gently. 'She's tired. I'm going to put her to bed early,' he said, and they offered not a murmur. Charlotte had acted like Lizzie Borden every time he tried to take me to the movies or dinner, and now she was totally unruffled by his saying he was going to put me to bed early. My entire family had been possessed by aliens, and Peter with them. But even my sanity was no longer certain.

They helped him rinse the plates and load the dishwasher, and then went back to their homework, after telling me they hoped I felt better. Neither of them seemed the least bit concerned that Peter appeared to have gone berserk. Worse yet, they seemed to like it.

'What did you put in their food? LSD? They're acting as crazy as you are.'

'I told you they'd love me. More than they

love him. Children sense it when someone genuinely cares about them. They respond to reality,' he explained gently as he reached into the fridge and pulled out a bottle of champagne I'd been saving for a special occasion. And this wasn't the one I'd envisioned.

'What are you doing?' He had opened it before I could stop him.

'Pouring us a little bubbly before we go to bed.' He smiled wickedly.

'Here? Now?' I was shrieking again, but I wasn't about to go to bed with him in the same house as my children. I had made that clear earlier and I thought Peter understood it. 'You can't go to bed with me here, Peter. You know that. Even in that outfit. I won't do it.'

'Relax. I'm going to stay in the guest room. We'll just sit and talk for a while, that's all. You need to unwind, Steph. You're all tensed up. It's not good for you to get so stressed out. Peter wouldn't like it. He sent me here to make you happy, not make you nervous.' But he had anyway. I had never been as nervous in my life or felt as disoriented. Paul had turned me topsy-turvy.

'Well, you're both crazy . . . you and Peter.'
I wasn't sure if it was the bourbon or the fact
that he was so convincing, but I was actually
beginning to think of him as another person.
'How can you do this to me?' He had turned
my life upside down in a single evening. And
what's more, my children didn't even seem to
mind it. But what were they going to tell
Roger when they saw him? That Mom had a
boyfriend who acted like a madman, and drank
gallons of bourbon? I'd lose custody over this
nonsense. But as I thought of it, and began to
feel hysterical again, he handed me a glass of
champagne, and was shepherding me toward
my bedroom door before I could stop him.

'Do you have any oil?'

'Why? Are you planning to drink that too?'
I was drinking the champagne by then. I wasn't
about to waste good champagne, and it was the
only way to cope with what had happened.

'I'm going to give you a massage,' he said
firmly as he closed the door to my bedroom,
and locked it.

'You're going to take those clothes off and
turn into who you really are again, that's

what you're going to do, Peter Baker.'

'Paul, darling. Paul Klone. And yes, I'll take my clothes off. But not till later. We don't want to upset the children.'

I finished the glass of champagne then, and before I knew it, he had unwound me like a cocoon, and I was lying naked on my bed, watching him, as he dug around in my bathroom cabinet and found some body lotion I had bought in Paris.

'This is perfect,' he said happily, as he returned, and took a long swig of champagne from the bottle. 'Do you have any candles?'

'Why?' I asked, in total panic. 'What are you going to do with them?'

'Light them. Candlelight will relax you. You'll see.'

'Nothing is going to relax me, ever again, if you don't stop this.' The time I was going to spend in Bellevue would be relaxing.

'Shh ... quiet ...' He dimmed the lights, and before I knew it, was massaging me with the French body lotion. I had no intention of succumbing to it, or to him, but it felt so good and I was so wound up, and had such a dreadful headache, that somehow I let him. And half an hour later, when the children came in, I was feeling dazed and wearing my dressing gown, sitting in front of the television, just the way I had before I met him.

'Feeling better, Mom?' Charlotte asked as she walked in, and then sheepishly asked Peter, or Paul as it were, to help her with her homework. They disappeared for over an hour, and by then I had put Sam to bed, and was beginning to think that things were returning to normal. Peter sounded like his old self as he went over algebra with Charlotte. And she was actually civil to him when she thanked him, and went back to her bedroom.

By ten-thirty, both children were in bed and sound asleep, and Peter was sitting in my bedroom, looking at me with a tender smile, as he took his shirt off.

'You can't do that. What if the kids wake up? Peter, you really can't sleep here.' I was near tears as I implored him.

'I told the kids that I was having construction done on my apartment, and you were kind enough to let me stay in the guest room for a couple of weeks. Neither of them seemed to have a problem with it, and Sam even asked me to sleep in his room.'

'What is happening to us? To you?' But whatever it was, it was working. It was the first time I'd ever had the feeling that Charlotte liked him. Maybe it was the outfit, or the dinner he cooked, or the way he was behaving, but he had suddenly won them over by wearing the worst clothes I'd ever seen, and behaving like a wild man. He was even moving into my guest room, and no one seemed to mind it. In fact, they were pleased about it.

He locked the door quietly, and as he slipped off the ghastly green pants, I almost felt as though I recognized him again, until I saw the gold lamé jockeys he was wearing, if you could call them jockeys. It looked more like a Speedo, and the gold was more than a little amazing.

'What is that?' I asked, laughing finally. He had taken the whole charade to the nth degree, and in a way, I almost had to admire him for it. It was crazy certainly, but maybe it was funny after all. You had to hand it to him for being creative.

'It's a G-string,' he explained, as I suddenly roared with laughter. I'm not sure if it was the G-string, or the champagne, but the whole thing suddenly seemed hysterically funny.

'I didn't think you had it in you to do this,' I said, as tears rolled down my cheeks while I laughed. 'You have a wicked sense of humor. I always thought you were so conservative.' In a funny way, I liked it. It had been an insane evening, but as he slipped out of the G-string, and tossed it in the air, I grinned at him, and found him more irresistible than ever. 'You are amazing . . .'

He took my dressing gown off then, lit the candles again, poured me a last glass of champagne, and proved to me that he was the man I knew and loved, and then some. He was more romantic, more loving, more sensual than I had ever known him, and did things to me I had only read about, or dreamed. It was as though the crazy game he had played with me all night had unleashed something wild in him that he couldn't have allowed himself otherwise. But as we lay in each other's arms afterward, I had no objections. It had been better than ever before, and I felt very free now.

'What did you say your name was?' I teased, smiling sleepily at him.

'Paul,' he whispered, as he kissed me again, and the phone rang.

'I love you,' I whispered back, and reached for the phone, before it could wake the children. It was nearly one o'clock in the morning.

'How did you like my surprise?' a familiar voice asked, as I looked around in confusion. It was Peter. But it couldn't be. He was in bed next to me, running a finger lazily down my spine as I listened. 'Is he behaving himself? Don't let him get too outrageous, Steph . . . or I'll get jealous.' My eyes opened wide as I listened to the voice on the phone. It was right out of *The Twilight Zone* as I turned to look at Peter, to make sure he was still there with me. But the voice on the phone was identical. I knew it too well, unless it was some crazed but very clever mechanical recording. But how could that be?

'Who is this?' I said, my voice a croak in my throat as I asked him.

'It's Peter. Isn't the Klone there with you?' I

looked at Paul then, and knew it was all true. Peter was in California. And Paul Klone was in my bed, had been making love to me as no one ever had before, and he'd been telling the truth all evening about not being Peter. But if he wasn't Peter, who was he? The room spun around me as I listened to him, and I looked at Paul, and unable to withstand anymore, I closed my eyes, and fainted.

Chapter Five

By the next morning, when I woke up, I realized with utter certainty that alien beings had taken over my life. I could hear Paul on the phone, as I opened my eyes, ordering five kilos of caviar, a case of Louis Roederer Cristalle, and another of Château d'Yquem. And before I could even comment on it, he had leaped across the room, talking about it being a great morning. But I was in no condition to discuss it with him.

I crawled out of bed, with an incredible hangover, something I hadn't had in years. It must have been the champagne. And as I stood in the shower moaning softly, trying to sort out what had happened, Paul came in and offered to help me shave my legs.

'No, thanks, I can do it myself.' He sat down on the toilet seat next to me then, with a fresh glass of champagne in his hand, while I wondered if I should just forget about my legs, and slit my wrists instead.

I still couldn't understand what had happened. I remembered talking to Peter supposedly in California the night before, but he was very clever and knowledgeable about technology. He had probably made the recording before he left, and it was actually him sitting there, next to me, drinking champagne, and pretending to be someone else. This clone story of his was more than a little far-fetched, but it allowed him to indulge in a lot of very exotic liberties and sex games and a most unusual style of dress, guilt-free. I wondered if it was the only way he could free himself of whatever inhibitions he had, and suspected that was it. But it really made me wonder what kind of neuroses he had to need to hide behind the pretense of being someone else. It was more than a little kinky, but at least I had worked it out in my head. The night before I had actually believed him for a while, but as he sat in my bathroom, watching me, wearing only a towel, it was easy to see that it was really Peter, no matter what name he wished to be called, or how outrageous the outfit.

'Feeling better?' he asked, as I stepped out of the shower, smiling finally. He wasn't going to fool me with his little game. And if that was the game he wanted to play with me, I could play it just as well.

'Much.' I kissed him, and took a sip of his champagne. 'That was fun last night,' I said drying my hair, noticing how handsome he was, by whatever name.

'I'm sorry it freaked you out a little bit when Peter called. It's a little startling at first, I realize, but once you adjust to the idea of it, it really makes a lot of sense. With Peter having to travel so much, he didn't want you to be alone. You know, it took them over three years to build me, and another year and a half just to get all the kinks out.' I wasn't quite as sure 'they' had. But we were apparently going to play 'Stephanie and Paul' today, and pretend that Peter was still away. 'What do you want to do today?' he asked amiably. 'After we get the kids off to school.'

'Don't you have to go to work?' I said hopefully.

'Eventually. It makes Peter a little nervous when I go into the office, but I feel guilty if I don't at least drop by every few days. But I thought today, we'd take the day off . . . and maybe just stay in bed.' He grinned at me outrageously, finished his champagne, and threw the glass away. But a little lost Baccarat was a small price to pay for a fantasy like this one.

'There's an exhibit I want to see at the Met . . . I mean after . . . that is if . . .' I couldn't believe I was blushing as I talked to him, but he smiled as he looked at me, and bent gently toward me to kiss my breast. 'Peter . . . don't . . .'

'Paul,' he whispered, and I nodded, and then tore myself away from him to get dressed. It was certainly an intriguing little game to play. It almost made me wonder what else he was into, whips and chains, handcuffs, or even more unusual costumes than the one he'd worn the night before. And as though to counteract the erotic fantasies I was beginning to have about him, I put on an old tattered gray sweater and my favorite pair of jeans. I slipped my bare feet into loafers, and walked soberly into the kitchen to feed the kids. Peter, alias Paul, had gone to make more phone calls, but he had promised to join us at breakfast, and see the children before they left for school.

I made waffles and bacon for everyone, since we had a 'guest,' and Sam had gobbled up all of his before Charlotte even left her room. She appeared late, as usual, straightening the much-too-short skirt she was wearing and fiddling with her hair. She was wearing a necklace that looked like a stop sign but said SEXY, and my favorite pair of high heels. And I sent her back to change into the Adidas she usually wore to school.

By the time she got back, she was even later, inhaled half a waffle, and informed me that eating bacon was sick. I nodded and picked up the paper, with a quick glance at my watch. It wasn't my day to drive them to school, and the mother who was scheduled to do it was almost always late. She already was, and as

I shook my head over it and picked up the business section, I felt as though an odd, almost other worldly presence had just entered the room. Unable to resist the forces around me, and sensing him before I saw him, I looked up. My eyes were instantly met with a vision that nearly defied description. For once, Sam was stunned into silence, and Charlotte whispered in awe, 'Too cool.' It was too something definitely. I'm not entirely sure 'cool' was the right word. 'Hot' might have been more like it.

The Klone, as he called himself, was wearing a one-piece leopard spandex jumpsuit, with a skintight T-shirt in an almost electric hot pink, with matching shoes. He had on sunglasses and a heavy gold necklace, and on his fingers he wore at least six enormous diamond rings. And as the sun streamed in on him, he looked as though he were going to explode in a million particles of blinding light, rather like a kaleidoscope enhanced by LSD. He was definitely 'too cool.'

'Bright in here, isn't it?' he said pleasantly, as he sat down at the table with a broad smile. All

I could do was stare at him. The outfit was beyond belief.

'I think it's just you,' I said, wondering if the khakis and conservative blue shirts had just been a ruse. Maybe this was the real him. If not, it was certainly an intriguing joke. But maybe he had just worn the conservative clothes to pull me in. In either case, this was sick, and I knew it.

'Anything special in the paper?' he asked comfortably, digging into his waffles and bacon, and pouring about an inch of maple syrup all over his plate, while Sam watched with glee and fascination.

'Would you like the fashion section?' I asked, as Sam warned him that all that sugar would rot his teeth.

'I hate the dentist,' he said amiably. 'Don't you?'

'Yeah,' Sam agreed, 'a lot. We go to a really mean dentist. He makes me use fluoride, and he gives me shots.'

'Then you shouldn't go, Sam. Life is too short to do things you don't like to do.' Sam nodded, in complete agreement, as I put the paper down slowly and glared at them both.

'Life is too long to spend it without teeth.' Peter's comment did not amuse me, nor did the look in Charlotte's eye when she asked him admiringly where he got the suit.

'It's Versace, Charlie. He's the only designer I wear. Do you like it?'

'More than life itself,' I volunteered for her, and then mercifully, the doorman called on the house phone. The car pool was downstairs to take them. 'Time for school!' I rushed everyone out the door, closed it, and then turned to look at him. 'What exactly are you trying to do? Cause a revolution here? They're children. They don't know you're just kidding . . . and Peter . . . that outfit . . .' I didn't know how to say it, but it wasn't going to be easy keeping Charlotte in anything even remotely respectable, if he kept wearing little numbers like this one.

'It's terrific, isn't it?' He grinned, and I sat down and groaned helplessly, and then looked up at him again. But he looked so sweet and so vulnerable, he actually looked hurt at the thought that I disapproved.

'Yes, it is terrific.' What the hell, he was brilliant, I loved him, he was great in bed, and the kids had left for school. What harm could it do if I played the game with him? If only for a day or two. He couldn't keep it up forever. No one could. Sooner or later, he'd get tired of teasing me, and he'd have to go back to the khakis and the Gucci shoes. But I was secretly longing for the days when Charlotte called him a dork because he was so conservative. The little leopard spandex number was certainly anything but.

But as I looked at him, he grinned mischievously, and pulled me out of my chair. 'Come on, Steph . . . let's go back to bed.'

'I have a million things to do today, and I haven't finished the paper,' I said sternly, as though that would dissuade him. Ever since Roger left, I had promised myself I would wear makeup every day, and keep abreast of the news.

'It's all the same crap that happens every day, every week,' he assured me, unmoved. 'People killing each other, people dying, guys making home runs and touchdowns, stock prices going up and down like yo-yos. So what? Who cares?'

'I do,' I laughed at him. He looked so ridiculous in that outfit, particularly with the huge gold chain around his neck. He looked like the Ghost of Christmas Past gone Hollywood. 'And so do you, unless all that spandex has gone to your head. You can't suddenly stop caring about the real world, just because you're playing a joke on me. The outfit is one thing . . . the rest is something else.'

'It certainly is,' he said, ignoring me completely, as he scooped me up in his arms like a Barbie doll and marched back to my room, where I had already diligently made my bed. He pulled it open with one hand, as his rings flashed in the sunlight, and deposited me lovingly on my Pratesi sheets. And without hesitating for a moment, he began to undress. Very conveniently, the leopard body suit had a concealed zipper, and in less than a second, he had unzipped it, and pulled it off, right over his electric pink shoes. And then he stood there in a leopard satin G-string, his hot pink T-shirt, and the matching shoes. 'Now talk to me about the stock market,' he said, as he slipped off the shoes and the necklace, and joined me in my king-size bed.

'I thought we were going to the Met,' I said breathlessly, as he began to undress me, but as he kissed me I found I was too overwhelmed by him to object. 'Do you think we should . . .' I whispered weakly. It was broad daylight, I was the mother of two children. What was I doing with a man in a leopard satin G-string, making love to him while they were at school? But as the G-string disappeared like so much dental floss, along with my blue jeans and pink lace undies, my objections seemed to vanish into thin air.

He was extraordinarily athletic, and even more sensual than he had been before. And then as I lay gasping in the throes of passion, he whispered in my ear.

'There's something I want to show you,' he said hoarsely, clearly as overcome with desire as he made me feel. I should have been afraid of him then, I should have sensed something wrong about him right at the beginning, in Paris, but it was too late to remember any of that now. He owned me as he held me close to him, my body one with his, as he rolled me slowly over and over and over. And the next moment, as we seemed to catapult into the air, all the air in my lungs was sucked out of me, as we somersaulted in midair, still coupled, did a neat little pirouette of sorts, and wound up artfully, almost gracefully, with me lying on top of him, on the floor. I couldn't believe he'd done it, had no idea how he had managed it, and not hurt me or himself. He was laughing and I was smiling, as he explained it to me. 'It's called a double flip, Steph . . . it's my specialty . . . Do you like it?'

'I love it.' I didn't even mind the fact that somewhere mid-maneuver, his castaway little leopard G-string had somehow caught on my left ear.

'I managed a triple once . . . but I didn't want to hurt you. I thought we should start slow at the beginning . . . and work up to a triple . . . even a quadruple . . . It adds something very special to a beautiful moment between two people, don't you think?'

'I do.' I was still more than a little breathless, and amazed we hadn't hurt each other. But he was unharmed and unruffled as he lifted me gently back onto the bed, and tried it again. We actually achieved a triple, sometime early that afternoon. We never made it to the exhibit of Old Masters at the Met, but by then I didn't care. I was living in Nirvana somewhere, suspended in a world of his creation, my body the instrument he played like a Stradivarius, or something very delicate and precious. And as we sank into the bathtub together afterward, all I could do was close my eyes and dream. I was so pleasantly exhausted, so sated and well loved, that I didn't hear the phone ring, and when I did, I didn't care.

'Steph . . . sweetheart . . .' he whispered, as I drifted slowly to earth again, and looked at him. 'You should answer the phone. It might be the kids.'

'What kids?'

'Yours.'

I couldn't have remembered their names at that point if he asked me, but I knew I should answer the phone. But he had cast a spell on me so powerful, he was all I could think of. Him, the triple flip.

'Hi, there.' A familiar voice sounded buoyant, and hearing him so energetic and alive, I winced. I looked straight at Peter in the tub across from me, and wondered how he did it. If it was a recording of his voice, the timing was very good. He was playing the phone game with me, but this time I knew I would catch him at his own game. I had figured out that morning that the way he did it was by having such an ordinary conversation with me that my answers would be entirely predictable. And I would never realize it was a recording, and not a real person on the phone, talking to me.

'Hello, Peter.' I played the game with a wink and a broad grin.

'How are you, Steph?'

'Pretty sexy,' was my answer, instead of 'fine.'

'What does that mean?' he asked. Another standard response to anything I might have said.

'I'm just lying here in the bathtub. We've been making love all afternoon.' There was a moment's pause, which made me smile. He had obviously left a space in the recording, which was clever of him.

'He's bionic, Steph. He's not real. He's entirely man-made, synthetic from head to toe, and he doesn't mean a thing he says. And whatever he does, it's strictly a mechanical performance.' From my experience, that made him fairly typical of his breed. Nothing unusual about that, or about what Peter was saying to me.

'We just did a triple flip.' Try producing a standard response to that. The conversation was slipping rapidly away from what Peter might have expected when he made the tape.

'He wasn't supposed to do that, Steph. He was just supposed to keep you entertained till I got back. That isn't what we programmed him for at this end. It sounds like things are getting out of control there.' He sounded worried and I grinned. The joke was on him now.

'I'd say things are very much "out of control" at this end.'

'You're making me jealous, Steph. You sound as though you think he's real.' He didn't sound pleased about it. In fact, he sounded almost sad, which unnerved me.

Touching vastly impressive parts of him gently with my foot beneath the water in the tub, I nodded with a mischievous grin. 'I believe he is real.'

'Well, he's not. We programmed him for that ridiculous little stunt, just for the hell of it, but I told him not to try it. He could hurt someone. Besides, I never expected him to do that with you.' This was not the standard answer I expected, and listening to Peter at the other end, I frowned.

'What did you just say?' I asked, feeling nervous suddenly, and staring at Paul in the tub with me, as he closed his eyes innocently, and looked as though he was drifting off to sleep. Maybe he was a ventriloquist, or, if nothing else, psychotic. A sociopath at the very least. But how could this be? This didn't seem like a recording I was talking to, it sounded much too real and much too worried.

'I said, he wasn't supposed to do any of that with you. I thought he'd just hang around with you and the kids, and amuse you. Besides, I told him not to try the double flip, or the triple, with you, or anyone, on this trip. The damn fool even talked about wanting to try a quadruple, in the tryouts. Steph, if he even looks like he's going to do that, get out of bed immediately or he'll hurt you. But it doesn't make me happy to know he's fully operative. He was only supposed to be partially operative with you.'

There had been nothing partial about what we'd been doing, and I felt suddenly immensely guilty. What's more, it really did sound like Peter on the phone and not a recording after all.

'Peter? Is that you?' And then, by sheer reflex, I prodded Paul nervously with my foot, and he woke up with a start and started talking to me at the same time. This was no trick. Unless he was feeding me magic mushrooms, and I had hallucinated the entire afternoon.

'Of course it's me,' he said, sounding a little tense. 'Look, Steph, I'm glad you're happy. I wanted you to have fun with him. But not quite as much fun as I think you're having. He's not real at least. Just think of him as a giant toy, a kind of talking blow-up doll to keep you amused while I'm out of town.' He was trying to be sensible and fair about it. After all, he had unleashed Paul on me.

'Peter,' I was starting to feel sick again, and my head was beginning to reel. 'I don't understand this. I don't know what happened . . . I thought it was a joke . . . that he was you.'

'He is. They cloned me. Actually he's a hybrid of sorts, a clone tempered by bionics. It's something very new I wanted to share with you. He's nearly perfect, except for a few minor kinks. Look, just enjoy him. Take him to parties. Let him play with the kids.' Was he kidding? Was it possible? How could he do this to me? Was he insane? Worse yet, was I? If not yet, I knew I would be soon. Paul was a clone 'tempered by bionics'? Maybe these were all dreams as the result of a major head injury from the double flip. It was beginning to seem that way to me.

'What about me? How could you do this to me? I don't love him, I love you.'

'I love you too. And you're not supposed to love him. He's just supposed to keep you company, while I'm away. But not quite as much company as he seems to be keeping.

'Where are you going to have him sleep now?' With all I'd said to him, it was obvious where he'd been sleeping up till then.

'In the guest room. He slept there last night, after . . .' I couldn't finish the sentence, having already described our sexual exploits, thinking that the voice on the phone wasn't real. I had been lured, tricked, into an obscene situation, and all I wanted now was to disappear into oblivion forever.

'Good. Keep him in the guest room. And stay away from that goddam double flip.' Christ, now he was jealous. With a body like his, and Paul's, what did he expect? Mother Teresa couldn't have resisted him, and as I listened to Peter, Paul reached out and touched me, and I found myself longing to try the forbidden quadruple flip. 'I'll be home in two weeks.' Suddenly, it sounded just a little bit too soon. What on earth had I gotten myself into, and who were these people? Clones . . . bionics . . . fully operative . . . double flips? I was trapped in a high-tech nightmare.

'I'll be here, sweetheart,' I said weakly. And then what? Would Paul disappear? 'How's work?' It was the only thing I could think of to say, other than to ask about the weather in California.

'Fine. Where is he now, by the way?' He still sounded a little worried, but it was his own damn fault. Klone indeed.

'He's here,' I said vaguely, as Paul lathered soap suds down my back, and erotically across my chest.

'Where are the kids?'

'At school. They'll be home soon.' Unfortunately. There was barely time to try for another triple flip. I didn't care what Peter said. I couldn't give up Paul now, even if he was bionic.

'I'll call you later,' he promised. 'I love you, Steph.'

'I love you too,' and what's more, I meant it. The Klone was fun, but I had only let myself give way to him because I thought he was Peter . . . in fact, I had been so sure. And now I had to face what I was feeling, and what I had done with him, bionic or not. Peter said he was a toy

. . . but what a toy he was! Never in my life had I had a toy like him.

'How was he?' Paul asked when I hung up. I was staring at him in confusion, as he lay looking at me in the tub.

'He's fine,' I said vaguely, thinking of everything he had said, with no idea how to make peace with myself, or the situation I was in. 'He said to say hello.' In fact, he hadn't but what else could I say? I was in way over my head, and I knew it.

'He hates that double flip. I think it just bugs him because he can't do it. He's always afraid I'm going to tear some wires, or blow out my fuses, especially on the triple flip.'

'I think you blew out mine.' I smiled, still having difficulty believing it was all true. But there was no hiding from it now. I knew it was, the conversation with Peter had convinced me, especially the fact that he was jealous. 'He said you weren't supposed to be fully operative,' I said, chiding him gently, sounding like I was scolding Sam about his homework, or the dog.

'I forgot,' Paul said, smiling broadly. 'Champagne does that to me.' We knew what it had done to me, certainly. And he appeared to be entirely without remorse about it. 'We'd better get dressed before the kids come home from school,' he said responsibly, as though to atone for the sins we'd committed. 'They're really nice kids.'

'Peter likes them too,' I said wanly, staring at him again. He was the perfect likeness, and such an exquisite imitation that no one would ever have suspected he wasn't real. 'What's it like?' I asked, unable to resist the question, but like Peter, he was bright, and quick.

'Being a Klone? I like it. It gives me a lot of freedom. He usually lets me do what I want. I get a lot of off-time when he's around, and a lot of fun when he's gone.' Not to mention a lot of sex whenever he wanted.

'Have you done . . . uh . . . this for him before? I mean like this?' I wondered how many of Peter's girlfriends he had slept with, how many afternoons like this there had been, when he'd been 'fully operative' instead of 'partial.'

'No,' he said, facing me squarely, looking hurt. 'I haven't. This is the first time I've visited a woman. But they've done a lot of rewiring and corrections on me lately. He's only used me in business till now, and on a few friends. Just like you, they thought it was all a big joke. They love me at his office, but he gets nervous when I go in. I made a couple of pretty sketchy deals for him last year. But this is the first time he's ever trusted me with anything as important as this.'

There were tears in his eyes as he said it, and in mine too. How had this happened to me? God only knew. It had been such a normal, innocent romance until Paul walked through my front door. I didn't know what to do. Paul had gotten under my skin in a terrifying way in a few brief hours, but it was Peter I was in love with. Of that I was still sure.

'This is the first time anything like this has ever happened to me, Paul,' a vast understatement at best. 'I don't know what to think, or what to do.' I couldn't stop myself. I started crying and he held me in his arms and gently stroked my hair. There was something so endearing about him, even if he was bionic.

'It's okay, Steph . . . it's new to me too. We'll work it out together . . . it'll be all right, I promise . . . he travels a lot.' What he said turned my tears into sobs. What was I going to do? It was like being involved with two men, one I knew and loved, or thought I did, the other totally outrageous, unbelievably sexy . . . but then Peter was too. It had been a cruel trick to play on me, and made Roger seem like a schoolboy. All this high-tech stuff was just too much to deal with, or even imagine. How was it possible? I was in love with a twisted genius, and sleeping with a bionic clone. Who would have believed me if I'd told anyone? Like those stories of ordinary people kidnapped by UFO's. I had a new respect for them, as I looked at Paul.

'I love you, Steph,' Paul said gently, as I continued to cry in his arms, overwhelmed by the situation I was in, 'at least I think I do. You make my wires hurt. Maybe that's what love is.'

'Where?' I was suddenly intrigued by what he'd said, and wanted to know more about him.

'Right here.' He pointed to the back of his neck. 'That's where most of the wiring is.'

'Maybe you hurt it with the triple flip.'

'I don't think so. I'm pretty good at it. I really think this is love.'

'Yeah, me too.'

'Come on, get dressed,' he said with a look of mischief in his eyes. 'Why don't we go out for dinner with the kids?'

I couldn't help smiling at him. He was such a sweet person, and it was obvious he loved the kids. He almost seemed like one of them, except thank God they didn't dress like him.

I put on my blue jeans then, and a black sweater, and a new pair of black suede loafers. And ten minutes before the kids were due home from school, Paul came out of his room. I could tell he'd gone to a lot of trouble dressing, and the effect he had achieved was impressive. It was a whole new look. Black patent leather jodhpurs, with a matching red patent leather jacket, a matching cowboy hat, a silver lamé shirt, and silver alligator boots.

'Too dressy for dinner?' he asked, seeming worried. It was obvious that he really cared about how he looked.

'Maybe a little, if we're just going out for hamburgers or pizza.' I hated to tell him that he looked like a fire hydrant, but then I saw a spark of genius light his eyes.

'Why don't we take the kids to "21"? They know him there. We'll get great service, and Sam would love the model airplanes in the bar.' Much as I loved him, and as impressed as I was with the double and triple flip, I couldn't imagine walking into '21' with him, looking like that. But I knew that if I said anything about it to him, he would be devastated and deeply wounded.

'Maybe I should just cook dinner here,' I said gamely.

'Steph,' he looked at me with eyes filled with love, 'I want to take you out and celebrate.' Celebrate what? That I was sleeping with two different men but they were the same . . . or were they? Something about him just touched my heart, no matter how agonized I was over my own situation. It really wasn't his fault, it was Peter's. But I wasn't angry at either of them. In some ways, I was a victim of Peter's genius, and the mad experiment he had created. But I sensed that there was no real malice behind it. Poor Peter had even been upset that Paul was unexpectedly fully operative and I was sleeping with him. We had all gotten more than we bargained for on this one.

'We really shouldn't take the kids out during the week,' I said to Paul gently, hoping to discourage him from taking us to '21' and causing a scene there.

'Now you sound like him.' For an instant, he looked annoyed, and two minutes later, the kids walked in. Sam gasped when he saw the silver lamé shirt, and Charlotte was visibly impressed by the black patent leather jodhpurs and silver boots.

And then Paul told them that he wanted to take them to dinner at '21.' The kids were thrilled, and their reaction fascinated me. Charlotte had thought he was a dork for wearing black leather Gucci shoes when she first met him. Now, in red and black patent leather, looking like a neon sign, she thought he was cool. Even more so when he let her try on all his rings. And if I wore a skirt that was so much as an inch too short, or God forbid, a fur hat in winter so my ears didn't freeze, she thought I was so embarrassing she wouldn't walk down the same street with me. How does one explain the perversity of a thirteen-year-old, or even begin to understand what constitutes acceptable to them? Clearly, Paul got it, and I didn't. He was one of them. And I wasn't.

And in spite of all my protests, Paul convinced the children that we should go out, and at seven-thirty we were riding in a limousine, on our way to '21,' while the kids poured themselves Cokes in the backseat. He was still wearing the patent leather riding habit, and carrying a fur coat in case it got cold. And I was wearing a little black dress, and a string of pearls. He tried to get me to wear something less conservative. He even dove into my closet and tried to pick something out for me, but he was disappointed by what he found there. He suggested I throw it all away, and start again. On Peter's American Express card.

'We have to go shopping for you next week. Steph, I love you, babe, but your wardrobe is really kind of dull.' Like my flannel nightgowns in days gone by, I could suddenly see my entire wardrobe ending up in the trash, or at the very least, at the Goodwill. Maybe Peter would come home from California to find me wearing leopard spandex just like Paul. It was something to think about as we rode downtown. The limo he had hired was white and three blocks long, the only one I'd ever seen with a hot tub on the back, in lieu of a trunk. Sam had said 'Wow!' the moment he laid eyes on it. And when I whispered that it might be a little much, Paul reassured me that he had charged it to 'him.' I was sure that Peter would be thrilled about it. But this was what he had sent him to us for, if not the triple flip. This assignment was to entertain us, and he was doing a fine job of it so far.

The service at '21' was excellent, as usual, the meal superb. And without hesitating for an instant, when Sam exclaimed over the little airplanes hanging over the bar, Paul got up on a stool and cut three of them down for him. And when the head waiter rushed over immediately, Paul just told him to put them on the bill. He bought a cute tote bag for Charlotte on the way out, and a bathrobe with '21' embroidered on it for me. We all had a great time, and several people stopped at our table to say hello, and Paul was adorable with them. He made lunch dates with two of the men for that week. They agreed to meet at the University Club, since Peter was a member there. I was sure that the leopard spandex number, or even the patent leather jodhpurs, would be a huge hit.

Everyone was in high spirits when we got home, and I was just putting Sam to bed when Peter called. Fortunately, I got the call before Charlotte did, or she would have been hopelessly confused. I no longer was. I was growing used to it, and although I missed Peter, we were all crazy about Paul. And I knew what was waiting for me that night. Another night of ecstasy in his arms, and perhaps, with luck, another triple flip, though I knew enough now not to tell Peter about it. He had put me in this situation, now I had to deal with it. For that aspect of it at least, it was no longer his problem.

'Hi, sweetheart, where've you been?' he asked cheerfully.

'We just got back from "21,"' I explained. 'We all had a great time.'

'The three of you?' he asked cautiously.

'No, four. We went with Paul. He wanted to take us out, and he really spoiled the kids. He gave Sam three of the planes over the bar, and bought me and Charlotte everything in sight.'

'And charged it to me?' The voice from California sounded a little weak.

'He said you told him to. Was that all right? The limo too.'

'Limo? What limo?' Peter sounded confused at his end.

'It had a hot tub on the back. Sam thought it was "rad."'

'I see.' There was a pause while Peter regrouped, and I began to see all the advantages the Klone offered all of us, even the kids. It had been a huge adjustment psychologically, but it was a great arrangement once you got used to it. And I was doing my best to adjust, for Peter's sake. Having a Klone had a lot of merits for everyone, especially me. I had someone to do things with, to go out with the kids with me, someone to talk to and rub my shoulders . . . and then of course there was the triple flip to contend with. In some ways, I felt very lucky. I was no longer dealing with life entirely on my own. He was a companion of sorts in Peter's absence, albeit an odd one. Although, ever since my admissions to him about my sexual exploits with Paul, Peter seemed to be getting cold feet about the project.

'You know, Steph, I'm not sure you should go out that publicly with him. A quiet dinner here and there, in little French restaurants on the West Side, an evening with a few friends. But "21" might be pushing it a bit. He's a little conspicuous, don't you think? Or was he wearing one of my suits?'

'Could be,' I smiled, 'if you have one with black patent leather pants, and a red patent leather jacket to match, with a silver lamé shirt.'

'Let me guess. Versace, right?'

'I think so. He was the perfect host. He's got lunch dates at the University Club with some of your friends this week. They stopped at the table to say hello, and he thought it would be nice to take them to lunch for you.'

'Oh, for chrissake, Steph. Tell him to cancel immediately, and stay out of my clubs. I sent him there for you, not to go crazy all over town.

I'm going to have to send him back to be rewired again if he doesn't watch out.' Peter seemed a little irritable and unusually uptight to me, but that was understandable. It had been a big day for all of us, filled with unusual discoveries and unexpected revelations.

'How's everything out there?' I asked pleasantly, hoping to calm him, as Paul wandered into the kitchen, where I was on the phone, and opened another bottle of champagne. He had already had two of it at '21,' but he insisted that his wiring was so good, it wouldn't affect him, although he had already admitted that it had affected his memory the night before. But he said that he was able to drink all night, and never feel it. In fact he seemed to prefer alcohol to food. Clearly a glitch in his system.

'It's fine,' Peter said. 'I can't wait to come home. I miss you.' And he sounded as though he meant it. In fact, he sounded lonely.

'I miss you too,' I assured him, as I took a sip of Paul's champagne. 'I can hardly wait till you come home.' But I regretted it as soon as I said the words, Paul looked so hurt. And with a look of apology, I blew him a kiss. But he left the room as soon as I did. I suspected he was jealous, but there wasn't much I could do about it.

'It won't be long,' Peter promised. 'Just make sure Paul behaves himself. I want to have a life to come home to when I get back . . . and you.'

'You will,' I promised. He was, after all, the reason all this had happened. But it was Peter I was in love with. At least I was sure of that much.

'I'll call you tomorrow night.' He sounded more relaxed by then.

I missed him more than ever when I hung up the phone, but Paul accused me of being maudlin again, and reminded me that that was why he was here.

'To keep your spirits up, Steph,' he said lovingly, as I joined him in my room. The kids had gone to bed, and now it was our time. Paul put some sexy samba music on, and lit candles on either side of my bed. 'Forget about him.'

'I can't do that,' I explained. 'You can't just forget someone you love, it doesn't work like that.' But it was something he knew little or nothing about. He had wires instead of a heart, man-made mechanisms and computer chips where his brain would have been. As Peter had reminded me, he was entirely manufactured and man-made. It was an extraordinary feat of engineering, as was the double flip, as he did it again and again and again, late into the night. And Peter seemed as remote and unreal as if he had been on another planet. I wanted to keep him in my head, to believe in his reality, to know that he was coming back, and remember how much I loved him. But as Paul made love to me again and again that night, quite brilliantly, I found that Peter in his khaki pants and Oxford shirts was becoming a dim memory much faster than I would have thought possible, and only the Klone seemed real now.

Chapter Six

The first two weeks I spent with Paul Klone were the most extraordinary in my life, and in a way, it is almost impossible to explain. I had never had as much fun with any man, or laughed as much, or been as happy, not even with Peter. I talked to him in California regularly, but he was beginning to sound remote. Every time he asked what we were doing, and I told him, he got upset. It was hard to believe by then that sending me the Klone had been his idea. He was constantly annoyed about him, although I had never again mentioned our sexual endeavors to him. But in spite of my discretion, I think he knew Paul too well, and suspected what we were doing, though he no longer asked me directly.

Paul took me out to dinner almost every night, to '21,' Côte Basque, La Grenouille, Lutèce. And after he actually conquered the quadruple flip, he bought me an incredible emerald-and-diamond bracelet. He bought it at Harry Winston, with a ring to match, and an emerald necklace at Bulgari two days later, 'just because he loved me.'

'How do you know?' I teased him, as he put the necklace on me. 'That you love me, I mean.'

'I know because my neck hurts.' It was a sure sign with him. The other things he felt were either due to wire stress, or problems in his mechanism that he was promising to have fixed as soon as he went back to the shop, once Peter was back. But that was a moment in time neither of us could bear to think of. We lived each day to the max, and tried to convince ourselves it would last forever. We never talked about Peter.

Paul had lunch often at Peter's club, when we didn't spend the day in bed, and I had to do errands or keep appointments. It was hard having an affair with him, and keeping the rest of my life in order. And out of a sense of sheer obligation, every few days, he went to Peter's office to make sure everything was all right there. He loved it. I didn't question why he went, although I suspected it made him feel important. People bowed and scraped and catered to him, just as they did to Peter when he was there. It was heady stuff for a simple Klone. And he loved running his meetings, and making corporate decisions at random. It was hard work for him, he mentioned more than once, but he felt he owed it to Peter to put in an appearance for him. After all, initially that was why Peter had built him, although Paul admitted to me sheepishly his business systems weren't complete yet. But he said coming home to me after a hard day at the office made him feel nearly human. He loved being with me, and I with him.

Amazingly, the kids adjusted to him remarkably, and seemed suddenly to have no problem with the idea that he was sleeping in our guest room. After Charlotte's earlier vigilance about our 'doing it,' she no longer seemed to care now

and asked no questions, perhaps because she
knew what the answer could be and didn't want
to hear it. I continued assuring them that we
were sleeping separately, though I'm not sure
even Sam believed that anymore, but neither
of them objected. And I forced Paul to go back
to the guest room every night after our long
sieges of passion. It was usually four or five in
the morning before he got there, and a mere
two or three hours until I had to cook breakfast.
I didn't get a lot of sleep while he was there, but
it was a sacrifice I was more than willing to
make, considering what the rewards were.

And it was on one of his trips back to what
we now called 'his room,' that Paul ran into
Sam at five o'clock in the morning. I hadn't
noticed when he left me that he wasn't wearing
the now familiar G-string, but had opted to
make the brief walk back to the guest room
naked. Had I seen that, I would have strenu-
ously objected, in case he ran into Charlotte.
But at that hour, he had been fairly sure that
they were both sleeping. And covering his
body was not always something he thought
about. Since all the parts were interchangeable,

and apparently he changed them regularly, he felt less intensely private about them than you or I would. I had to remind him more than once to wear clothes to breakfast, as he prepared to breeze from the room without so much as his G-string. He seemed to view his collection of Versace as art more than an obligation to be decent.

In any case, he ran into Sam at five A.M. in the hallway. Apparently, Sam had had a bad dream and was on his way to find me, but ran into Paul instead, sauntering happily toward the guest room. I heard voices through the haze he'd left me in, and I peeked through the door to see my son looking up at Paul, who stood there, smiling at him, naked.

'How about a game of Monopoly?' Paul offered valiantly, as Sam stared at him in amazement. They played for hours, much to Sam's delight. The rest of us hated it, and Sam was so relieved to find someone to play it with him, he didn't even mind the fact that Paul cheated each time they played it. Sam beat him anyway, but this time he only guffawed at the offer.

'Mom would get real mad at us . . . I have school tomorrow.'

'Oh . . . what are you doing up then?'

'There was a hippopotamus under my bed,' Sam explained with a yawn. 'It woke me.'

'Yeah. That happens to me too sometimes. You've got to leave salt and half a banana under your bed. They hate salt and bananas scare them.' He said it with complete authority, as I debated whether to leave them alone or enter into the conversation. But I didn't want Sam to know that I was up, or that we'd been together.

'Really?' Sam looked impressed. He'd had the hippopotamus dream for years. The pediatrician had told me he'd outgrow it. 'Mom says it happens if I drink too much soda before I go to bed.'

'I don't think so . . .' Paul said thoughtfully, and then looked at him with concern. For a minute, I was afraid he'd offer him a bourbon, but he'd been pretty good about not doing anything like it so far, although he drank enough of it himself to refloat the *Titanic*. 'Are you hungry?' he offered instead, as Sam pondered the question and then nodded. 'Me too. How about a salami sandwich, with pickles, and peanut butter?' It was a concoction they had devised together, and Sam's eyes lit up at the suggestion. And with that, Paul put an arm around him and began heading for the kitchen.

'You'd better put some clothes on,' Sam suggested helpfully. 'My Mom might wake up and come to see what we're doing, and you'll scare her if she sees you like that. She doesn't like anyone walking around naked, not even my dad when he lived here.'

'Okay,' Paul said, and disappeared into his bedroom for an instant, only to emerge in a fuchsia satin bathrobe with purple tassels and yellow pom-poms that even Gianni Versace would have balked at creating.

And with that, I saw them turn the corner in the hall and disappear toward the kitchen. I left them alone, satisfied that they would share a private moment over the salami sandwich they made. It was good for Sam in a way to have a man to talk to, even if he was bionic. I felt certain that nothing untoward would happen, and went back to bed to catch up on the little sleep still left to me before I had to make Paul's favorite waffles for breakfast. And in the morning I inquired innocently about the salami rinds in the sink and the open jar of peanut butter on the counter.

'Did someone get hungry last night?' I asked, as I put a plate of bacon between Paul and Sam. As usual, Charlotte was still dressing.

'Yeah, we did,' Sam confessed easily. 'The hippo was back under my bed, and Peter made me a sandwich. He said to leave half a banana under my bed, the hippo'll be scared of it and he won't come back.' Sam sounded in control of his fear of it for the first time I could remember.

'And salt . . . don't forget the salt,' Paul reminded him, 'it's the salt they're really scared of.' Sam nodded thoughtfully, and then smiled up at him for a long moment, as I watched them.

'Thanks, Peter,' he said softly. Paul hadn't told him how silly he was. Instead he had offered tools, however absurd, to fight it. And it might just work, I knew, if Sam believed him, and he appeared to.

173

'It works, you'll see,' Paul reassured him, and then dove into his waffles, explaining why waffles were better for you than pancakes, because the little squares were filled with vitamins, even though you couldn't see them, and all the vitamins fell out of pancakes when you flipped them. Listening to him, I almost believed him, and even tired as I was, I loved the sound of Sam's laughter.

Paul was great with the kids, he was one of them, and his patience with them was endless. He took them out on the weekend, and played with them tirelessly, took them to the movies, and went bowling with Sam. He even went shopping with Charlotte, which was pretty scary and resulted in the purchase of a patent leather miniskirt I vowed to burn when he left us. They were absolutely crazy about him.

But at the end of the second week, knowing it would all be over soon, he started getting depressed and very quiet. I know Paul was thinking about leaving. He was going through cases of Cristalle, Yquem, and bourbon. But he held it remarkably well, and because of his delicate mechanisms, he never got hangovers and

was immune to headaches. The only sign of
drinking excessively he ever showed, was
when he got in a little accident on Third
Avenue in Peter's Jaguar. He managed to hit a
cab, and careened away from it, narrowly
missing a truck parked outside Bloomingdale's,
and hit six parked cars and a traffic light. No
one got hurt, but he totaled the front of the car,
and managed not to injure the trunk, where he
was carrying three more cases of Château
d'Yquem. He felt just awful about it, and didn't
want me to tell Peter when he called, so I didn't,
out of loyalty to him. He said the car needed a
new paint job anyway, the silver was so
mundane. In spite of his fondness for silver
lamé shirts and underwear, he thought it was a
poor choice of color for a car, and had it
repainted canary yellow. He swore to me that
Peter would be much happier when he saw it.
And he had the wheels painted red, which was
sweet of him.

It was an interlude in my life filled with
ecstasy and thrills I'd never before dreamed of,
and on our last night, at the thought of leaving
me, he was too depressed to even try the

double flip. He said his neck hurt too much. He just wanted to lie in bed with me, and hold me. He talked about how lonely it would be for him now, going back to the shop. He said it just wasn't going to be the same for him anymore, and I couldn't disagree with him. As much as I had missed Peter, I couldn't imagine living without Paul now. It was a time of roller-coaster emotions for both of us that were deeply confusing. I wondered if Peter would even mean as much to me now. In two weeks, Paul had done everything he could to broaden my horizons. He had even bought me a gold lamé minidress with cutouts for my breasts. He wanted me to wear it to dinner at Côte Basque, but I never got the chance. And although I didn't want to admit it to him, I think I was saving it for Peter. It was the only thing I saved. The rest had been liberally shared with both of them.

The last morning was the true test, because he couldn't say good-bye to the kids. We both understood that it wasn't possible for them to know that there were two people involved with me, or rather one, and a Klone. They had to think it was the same person coming home that night when Peter arrived. I made waffles for Paul for the last time, for now at least, and instead of syrup, he smothered them in bourbon. He was crazy about my waffles.

And then the final moment came. I helped him pack, all the silver and gold lamé, the chartreuse velour jeans, the spandex suits in zebra and leopard. Touching each of them brought back memories for me, and looking at him nearly tore my heart out.

'Leaving you is the hardest thing I've ever done,' he said with tears rolling slowly down his cheeks, and for an interminable moment, I held him close to my heart. So much so that his diamond peace sign was embedded in my chest and left a mark there.

'You'll be back,' I whispered, fighting back tears, 'he'll go away again.'

'Soon, I hope,' he said, sounding distraught. 'I'll be so lonely in the shop without you.' He was going to be in a lab in New York this time, but when I asked if I could come and visit him, he shook his head. 'They take me apart, and rewire everything each time,' he said. 'I don't want you to see me that way. They rebuild my body and take my head off.' It was an image I still found hard to adjust to.

'Make sure they don't change anything I love,' I said, smiling at him, and he grinned at me then, mischief dancing in his eyes again. I'll never forget that moment. He was wearing fuchsia satin pants, and a yellow vinyl shirt with rhinestone polka dots on it.

'They can rebuild anything you want smaller or bigger,' he said, 'there are endless options.'

'Don't change a thing, Paul. You're perfect as you are,' I reassured him. And then, without saying a thing, he closed the purple alligator suitcases they'd made for him at Hermès, and walked slowly to the door of my apartment, and then stopped to look at me.

'I shall return,' he said victoriously, and we both smiled knowing it was true, or hoping so at least. And then he was gone, and I was left alone in the empty apartment to think about him, and the quadruple flip. It was hard not to think about it.

I had exactly two hours to compose myself, to readjust, to try and turn my thoughts from

him, and turn my mind, and heart, back to
Peter. He had asked me to pick him up at the
airport, and I wasn't sure I could do it. It wasn't
easy going back to Peter, after Paul. The Klone
had made a lasting impression on me. And I
was no longer sure what Peter meant to me
now. My two weeks with the Klone had literally
changed my life, and I knew it.

I took a bath thinking of Paul, and the time
we had spent talking there, and I took out a
photograph of Peter to remind myself of what
he looked like. They were identical, of course,
but there was something in Peter's eyes, in his
heart, that was very different and spoke to my
soul. And then I had to remind myself that Paul
was only a Klone, a mass of wires and computer
parts that had been brilliantly made, but he was
not real. And in truth, however much fun I'd
had with him, he was not Peter. I was slowly
returning to earth now.

I put on a new black suit from Dior, and a
hat, and looked at myself in the mirror. I
looked so dull, almost as dreary as I had in the
old, flannel nightgowns in days gone by. But to
cheer myself up, I put on the new diamond

bracelet and the ruby pin Paul had bought me just before he left, with matching earrings. They were from Van Cleef, and as he always did, he charged them to Peter. He was sure he'd be happy to know he'd bought me something I was so fond of.

I was still feeling subdued in the limo on the way to the airport. Paul had tried to convince me to rent the white one with the hot tub on the back, but I had the feeling Peter might be happier with a smaller black one. I just couldn't see him using the hot tub, although Paul had, and loved it.

The plane was late, and I stood at the gate for half an hour waiting for Peter, still wondering how I would feel when I saw him. It was hard to say after the two weeks I had just spent with Paul. I wondered if everything would be spoiled now. I hoped not.

And then, as I waited breathlessly, as people in track suits and jogging shorts and boxers began filing out, I saw Peter. He was slim and tall, with a new haircut and a serious air, and that incredibly powerful way of walking. He was wearing a double-breasted blazer and gray slacks, a blue shirt of course, and a Hermès tie with a navy background and tiny yellow dots. And just watching him move toward me took my breath away. This was no imitation, no Klone, this was the real thing, a real man, and I felt my heart pound as I watched him approach me. I could tell in an instant that nothing had changed between us. Much to my own surprise, I loved him more than ever. It was hard to explain, especially after the fun I'd had with the Klone. But Peter was real, and Paul wasn't.

We talked endlessly on the way home, about life, and the kids, his work, and everything he'd done in California in the past two weeks. He never asked about Paul once, or how it had all worked out, or when he'd left. The only thing he wanted to know was why I had come to the airport in a limousine, instead of his Jaguar. And I had to explain that Paul had had a little mishap with it. I assured him that they had put out the fire in the engine immediately, and other than the totaled front end, there had been very little other damage. The trunk still opened easily, all the tires were being replaced, and he was going to love it canary yellow with red wheels. I saw a muscle tighten in his jaw, but to his credit, he said nothing about it. He was a gentleman, and a good sport, as he always had been.

He seemed happier to see me when we got home. He left his bags in the car, but came up for a while, for a cup of tea. And then he kissed me. And when he did, I knew nothing had changed between us. Peter kissing me was more powerful than the double or triple or quadruple flip with Paul. Just seeing him again turned my knees to mush. I was crazy about him.

He went back to his own place then, to shower and change, and when he came back that night to see me and the kids, they both looked disappointed when they saw him come through the door. He was wearing jeans, a blue Oxford shirt, a navy cashmere sweater, and the Gucci loafers. I had to remind myself that this was Peter, and not Paul, and my days of leopard spandex and gold lamé were over for the time being. I tried not to think of Paul, with his head off in the shop. More importantly I had lost my head over Peter again, though I had no regrets about Paul.

And while I was fixing him a martini in the kitchen, Charlotte came in and whispered, 'What happened to him? He hasn't looked like a dork in weeks. And now look at him.' But the truth was I loved the way he looked, better than G-strings, and spandex and purple cowboy hats. I loved his 'dork' look, and thought it irresistibly sexy and very 'cool.' But that was hard to explain to Charlotte, who preferred the fluorescent green jeans, and the fuchsia satin overalls he had promised to lend her.

'He's just tired, Char,' I explained vaguely. 'Maybe he's in a quiet mood. Maybe he just had a bad day at the office.'

'I think he's schizophrenic,' she said bluntly. Possibly. Or maybe I was. That was also an option.

But they were even more surprised to learn that he had moved back to his own apartment again. I explained that the construction he was doing there was going so well that he no longer needed our guest room, now at least. And Sam looked heartbroken to hear it.

'You're not staying here?' he asked miserably, and Peter shook his head.

'I moved back to my apartment this morning,' Peter explained, sipping the martini, and playing with the olives.

'It must be Mom's cooking,' Sam said, shaking his head, as he went back to his own room. It was an adjustment for everyone, especially me, as we sat on the couch holding hands, and finally snuck into my room once we knew the kids were asleep. Out of sheer habit from the last two weeks, I lit the candles on either side of my bed, and Peter raised an eyebrow.

'Isn't that dangerous?' he inquired, looking worried.

'I don't think so . . . it's pretty.' I turned to face him, and he was watching me cautiously. I knew we were both wondering the same thing. What would it be like now?

'You're beautiful, Stephanie,' he said softly. 'I missed you while I was away.' And I could see from the look in his eyes that he meant it.

'So did I,' I said in a whisper in the candlelight.

'Did you?' He looked worried, but as though he wanted to believe it was true, and it was. I loved him even more now. 'It wasn't the same here without you.' An obscene understatement. But I had missed him. Terribly. Just seeing him standing there again, I was reminded of all that we had together. And then he reached for me ever so gently, and pulled me closer to him, and as he did, all else was forgotten, as though Paul faded from my memory the moment Peter touched me and erased a whole block of information and feelings. It was very odd, and I didn't understand it.

Peter was everything I had always known him to be, tender, loving, artful, considerate, sensual, an extraordinary lover in every way. There were no acrobatic twists and turns, no double flip, no triple, or quadruple. There were only the two of us, transported to a place I had nearly forgotten in the past two weeks. And as I lay in his arms afterward, he gently stroked my hair and then kissed me.

'God, I missed you,' he said, and I smiled.

'I missed you too . . . so much . . . it was a crazy time.' But in a way, although I didn't realize it at the time, it had shown me how much I loved him. He didn't ask about Paul then, or what we had done together. I sensed easily that he didn't want to know, although I was sure he suspected. Sending Paul to me was something he had done for me, a kind of gift from him, but in his mind, it was over. In mine, it was something I would have to live with, and absorb. But it was Peter who was important to me, who was a part of my real life, not the Klone. And wherever Paul was now, I knew they had already taken his wires apart, and his head off.

'You looked beautiful when you picked me up today,' Peter said peacefully in the flickering candlelight. 'Where did you get all those rubies? Were they real?' They had been extraordinary, but he'd been so excited to see me that he'd forgotten to mention them.

'They're from you.' I smiled, looking up at him, as I lay against his shoulder. 'Paul bought them for me, at Van Cleef. They're pretty, aren't they?'

'Did he charge them to me?' Peter asked, trying heroically not to look as stunned as he was. I nodded, and felt him grow anxious as we lay side by side.

'He said he knew you'd want me to have them. Thank you, sweetheart.' I nestled closer to him, and felt his tension as he lay next to me, and he said nothing more about the rubies. 'I love you, Peter,' I said gratefully, remembering the miraculous things he had just done to me. It was good to have him home again, better than it ever had been.

'I love you too, Steph,' he whispered. And I knew that, wherever he was, and whether or not he would return again, in his own loving, inimitable way, Paul Klone had brought Peter even closer to me.

Chapter Seven

The next three months with Peter were remarkable, in their own way, the children readjusted to him, although they wondered what happened, after his brief two-week fling at near insanity and wearing cool clothes. But they got used to the Gucci shoes again, and so did I.

Peter and I spent a lot of time together, and I had never been as happy in my life as I was with him. We went to movies, plays. I met all his friends, and I liked most of them. He spent weekends with me, whenever the children went to stay with their father. And I spent the occasional night at his apartment, when I had a sitter for the kids, and left at six A.M. to come home to make breakfast for them, still smiling from my nights with Peter.

I fell in love with him more each day, in spite of his occasional cool spells, and his occasional doubts about being involved with me, which I think came from years of independence and being on his own. According to him, I was the first serious relationship he'd had in many years. His freedom was important to him. He was actually very different from Paul. In contrast, Paul seemed to have very little need for freedom. But Peter was another story. He had been single for a long time, and in some ways, I suspected that commitment wasn't easy for him anymore.

But in spite of that, the relationship seemed solid. It meant a great deal to me, and it was obvious that it did to Peter as well. It was a more meaningful relationship than I'd ever had with anyone, including and perhaps even especially, Roger. This was real, as real as it could be, with ups and downs, and laughter, and occasionally tears, and the shared confidences that we trusted each other with, and there were many of them. And although I'd had doubts about him when he sent the Klone to me, I decided finally that although he was perhaps unusual, Peter was, in fact, normal and very sane. The Klone was simply an added facet to him. And of course, like all men, he needed to remind me from time to time that there were parts of him I didn't know yet, and still other parts that I might never know. It added a veil of mystery he seemed to feel was important, but the truth was that I saw who he was, and he had fewer secrets from me than he wanted to believe. I was willing to accept that there were some small, dark, hidden parts he had kept to himself, but they didn't frighten me. What I saw and what I felt and what I knew was a kind, generous, sensitive, intelligent, loving man. And he proved it to me in a thousand ways.

He was always patient and loving with my children, and had a special kind of empathy and tenderness in handling Sam. He was tolerant and understanding of Charlotte's moods and quirks as well, and the fact that some days she liked him, and at other times she wouldn't even say hello. I scolded her if she was rude to him, but he then chided me in turn for my lack of compassion, and was always quick to explain to me why this wasn't easy for her, and I had to back off, and give her a chance to get to know him in her own time.

But it was with Sam that he particularly touched me in late October. It was in fact on Halloween, and I had been putting together a Batman costume for him. Roger had promised to take him to a Halloween party, and there was no way I could take him, because I had promised myself to Charlotte that night, as a chaperone at her school dance. And it was important to her that I be with her. If they didn't have enough chaperones, they had threatened to cancel the school dance, and my canceling out on her could put the whole event in jeopardy, since most of the other parents didn't seem to want to go. I had sworn to her that, no matter what happened, I would be there. But at the last minute, Roger called, and said Helena was sick and he couldn't take Sam out after all. I explained to him that he *had* to, but he said Helena would never understand how important it was, they thought she had appendicitis, and I would have to make other arrangements for Sam on my own. Peter sat listening quietly on the couch, as I battled futilely with Roger on the phone.

I sat for a long quiet moment, wondering what to do, and what I was going to tell Sam. I was already signed up at Charlotte's school, and she was in her room, dressing for the dance. Backing out on her at the last minute would be a sin she would never forgive me for, but making Sam stay home with a sitter on Halloween would break his heart.

I glanced across the room at Peter, with despair in my eyes.

'I take it Roger can't make it?' He looked at me sympathetically as I nodded, silently running through the options in my mind. I was wondering if a sitter could take Sam to his party, but it was too late to find one, and I knew Sam better than that. He would opt not to go, and I knew how important Halloween was to him. I needed to be two people, and unlike Peter, there was no way out for me. I didn't have a Klone.

'They think Helena has appendicitis,' I

explained with a morbid look. 'Christ, couldn't she have done that some other time?'

Peter walked across the room to me with a gentle smile and a warm look in his eyes. 'I'll take him, if he'll have me. I don't have anything else to do tonight.' He had been planning to have dinner with friends, while I went to Charlotte's dance. And the truth was, I didn't know if Sam would have him. He had expected to go with his father, and although he liked Peter, going out with the man in my life on Halloween wasn't quite the same. 'Why don't I ask him?' Peter said matter-of-factly. 'If it's okay with him, I'll cancel my other plans.' I knew he was fond of the people he was meeting and they were only in town from London for a couple of days, and this was the only free night they'd had. But there was no question in my mind, I needed his help.

'Let me ask him first,' I said gratefully, and stopped to kiss him. 'Thank you for doing it . . . I know it'll mean the world to Sam.'

But when Sam heard what had happened, he was too disappointed to be reasonable. He didn't care what Peter had offered, he was

furious with Roger, and so disappointed he
wadded his Batman costume up in a ball, and
threw it on the floor.

'I'm not going,' he said, throwing himself on
his bed, with tears of defeat and sorrow running
down his face. 'Dad always goes out with me
on Halloween . . . it won't be the same.'

'I know, sweetheart . . . but it's not his fault if
Helena is sick. And he can't just go out and
leave her. What if she has to go to hospital and
he's not there?'

The voice from the depths of his pillow was
muffled, but audible nonetheless. 'Tell her to
call 911.'

'Why can't Peter take you?'

'He's not my father. Why can't you?' Sam
said, rolling on his back to look at me mourn-
fully, the tears still fresh on his face.

'I have to go to Charlotte's dance.' And as I
said the words, I saw the door open, and Peter
take a single cautious step into Sam's room. He
stood there hesitantly for a moment and looked
straight at Sam, man to man, and asked a
respectful question.

'May I come in?' Sam nodded, but didn't

answer as Peter made his way slowly to Sam's bed, and sat down on the end of it, as I quietly left the room, praying that Peter would know the right things to say.

I'm not entirely sure what happened after that, except that Sam told me many days later that Peter's father had died when he was ten, and his mother had had to work very hard to support him and his younger brother. There had never been anyone to go places with him. But he had been very close to the father of his best friend. He had gone fishing with them, and camping, and skiing once. And for the father-son camping trip, his best friend's father had taken both of them. It hadn't been the same for Peter either, but to this day, he had told Sam, as my son relayed to me later on, he and his best friend's father were still friends. He went to Vermont, where he lived now, every year to see him, and it means more to him than ever, because the man's son, Peter's friend, had been killed in Vietnam.

Sam had obviously been impressed by the story, because half an hour later, he appeared in my room with Peter standing beside him, his

Batman costume on, and a look of resignation on his face.

'Peter said he'd go as Robin,' Sam announced, 'if you've got anything for him to wear.' No problem, one Robin costume coming right up, twenty minutes before I had to leave for the dance. Of such minor challenges motherhood is made. We made holes for him to see through in an old sleep-mask I'd taken from an airplane. I found an old gray sweatshirt, and a black wool cape, and he actually looked pretty credible, even in his gray flannels. I somehow couldn't see him leaving the building in gray tights, even if I had had some, which thank God, I did not. And for a moment, as I looked at him before they left arm in arm, Peter reminded me more of the Klone than of himself. Paul would have had the tights, of course, and a pair of Versace boots to match, but Peter's gray slacks and loafers looked just fine. I kissed them both before they left, thanked Peter, and rushed back to my room, to comb my hair and change my dress for Charlotte's dance.

'You're late, Mom!' She glowered at me from

the doorway five minutes later, as I simul-
taneously slipped on my shoes and zipped up
my dress.

'No, I'm not,' I said breathlessly, grabbing
my handbag, and smiling at her. There was no
doubt whatsoever in my mind, Peter had saved
the day.

'What have you been doing?' It would have
taken too long to explain. She seemed to
assume I'd been eating bonbons and watching
my favorite show on TV.

'Nothing,' I said modestly, just salvaging
Sam's Halloween for him and dressing Peter as
Robin. No big deal. I did things like that every
day.

'Come on, we can't be late,' she said,
handing me my coat and bag as we rushed out
the door

As it turned out, we weren't. We caught a
cab immediately, and I reported for duty as a
chaperone at the scheduled time. Charlotte had
a great time at the dance, and when we got
home, Peter and Sam were sitting on the couch,
chatting like old friends. They had already
made their way through several Hershey bars,

four packs of Rolos, and there were silver papers from Hershey's Kisses and orange Kit Kat wrappers spread all over the couch. But in addition to the stomachache they were soon to share, it was obvious that a new bond had formed, and once again, Peter had won my heart.

'How was it?' I asked as Charlotte disappeared down the hall, having thanked me adequately for taking her to the dance.

'It was great! Peter and I are going to the Princeton-Harvard game,' Sam announced proudly. 'And he said he'd take me on the school ski trip, if Dad can't go.' Peter looked over his head into my eyes, and I saw something there I had never seen before, something tender and open and very warm. Whatever reservations Peter may have had about making a commitment to me, Sam had made serious inroads into his heart that night. It was a look that, however developed the technology, could never have been cloned.

And when I went to kiss Sam in bed that night, he lay smiling up at me from his pillow. 'He's a great guy,' he said about Peter, and all

I could do was nod, and fight back the lump in my throat.

'I love you, Sam,' I whispered softly.

'I love you, too, Mom,' he said with a sleepy yawn. 'Thanks for a terrific Halloween.'

Peter and I talked for a long time that night, about his childhood, and the death of his father, and then his mother when he was fourteen. In a way, he was an odd and lonely man, more so than I had ever realized, and it explained why he was so cautious about getting too attached to anyone. I think he was afraid that if he came to love us too much, something terrible might happen and he might lose us. But whatever fences he had built around himself over the years, it was obvious that Sam had broken right through them that night, dressed as Batman on Halloween.

'I think I had more fun than he did tonight. He's a great kid.' Peter smiled lovingly at me, and pulled me closer to him on the couch.

'He said pretty much the same thing about you before he went to sleep, and I agree with him. Thanks for saving the day for us. Better than that. Thanks for saving my life.'

'Anytime,' he swept a quick bow from where

he sat on the couch, 'Robin at your service.' He kissed me then, and his kisses tasted of Hershey bars and Kit Kats. I like that in a man. There was a lot I liked about Peter that night, and I fell in love with him all over again.

I met Peter's son on Thanksgiving, who was appropriately suspicious of me, and as rude as he dared to be, which was comforting. It reminded me of Charlotte with him in the beginning. She had long since come to the conclusion that Peter was boring, but harmless. And Sam truly liked him, especially after Halloween.

It was in early December that Peter told me he was going back to California for two weeks again. He hadn't been there in nearly three months. And as he said it, I was almost afraid to ask the obvious question. He didn't volunteer anything, and I didn't dare ask. I took him to the airport in the Jaguar, which had been repainted, *again*, by then. He had had it restored to silver. Its brief moment of canary yellow never saw the light of day. He never let it leave the shop that way, which somehow seemed a pity to me. Paul had thought it a terrific color, and had chosen it carefully, thinking Peter would like it. But as in everything else, nothing but their looks were the same.

Peter kissed me lovingly when I left him at the airport, and told me not to be lonely, and keep busy while he was gone. There was a slew of early Christmas parties we were invited to, and he urged me to go to all of them. I told him I wasn't sure I wanted to and mulled it over, as I drove back into the city. I didn't want to go to the parties without him. I was almost sorry he hadn't sent me the Klone this time, or promised to. I missed the Klone. It would have been a good time to have him around. But the last visit obviously had bothered Peter. And this time as he left, Peter said nothing about the Klone coming to see me, and I didn't ask. I think Peter was sorry about ever sending me the Klone in the first place. He had never mentioned him again, and I'd gotten the impression that he felt the first visit had gotten out of hand.

I was cooking dinner for the kids that night, when the doorman buzzed and said something had arrived, so when the doorbell rang, I sent

Danielle Steel

Sam to answer to see what it was, and he returned to the kitchen with a broad smile.

'What is it?' I had told him not to open the door until he looked through the peephole.

'It's not what, it's who,' he said with a knowing look, and then was quick to explain. 'It's Peter, he's back, and he looks like he's in a good mood again. I guess he didn't go to California after all.' Just listening to what Sam said, I wondered. I put the spatula down that I'd been brandishing, and ran to the door, still in my apron. I was wearing jeans and an old sweater. I opened the door, and then I saw him standing there, with stacks of purple alligator suitcases all around him. It was Paul, and he was beaming at me. He had clearly conned the doorman into letting him come up unannounced. He always tipped them well.

He was wearing chartreuse satin disco pants, and a mink jacket, and peeking through it I could see no shirt at all, only his bare chest, and his diamond peace sign shimmering at me.

'Merry Christmas!' were the first words he said to me, and then he kissed me with unbridled passion.

'Wow!' I whispered, looking him over carefully. He hadn't changed a bit in three months. It could have been Peter, but I knew it was Paul, back from wherever he had been to have his wires polished up, and his chips replaced. God only knew what they did now. But I was thrilled to see him. 'How have you been?' I suddenly realized how much I had missed him. More than I would ever have admitted to Peter, or even to myself.

'I've been bored as hell, thanks a lot. I spent three months with my head off. I didn't even know he was going away again. They just told me this morning. I came as soon as they called.'

'I think he decided on short notice,' I whispered. And I was happier to see him than I knew I should be. The last three months with Peter had been wonderful . . . but Paul brought with him something magical, and very different. A kind of madness blessed by outrageous spirits and kissed by elves. He was wearing yellow alligator cowboy boots, and when he took the mink jacket off, I could see he had on a tiny black see-through undershirt, covered in rhinestones. He looked very festive, and happy to see me.

He hugged both of the kids, and Charlotte rolled her eyes at him, and said, 'Now what? Are you on one of your crazy kicks again, Peter?' But she grinned at him. She liked it when he got a little crazy. And Sam giggled at the outfit, as Paul poured himself half a glass of bourbon. This time he knew where I kept it, and took it out of the cupboard with a grin, and a wink at the kids.

'Are you staying with us again?' Sam inquired, looking amused. The last time 'Peter' had looked like that, he had stayed in our guest room for two weeks. He thought the yellow cowboy boots were a little silly. But Peter was his buddy, and had been for months, in khaki pants, or chartreuse satin. They were growing accustomed to what they thought were his mood swings and his fluctuating taste in clothing. And as though to confirm that to me, Charlotte whispered to me when he walked out of the kitchen with Sam.

'Mom, he needs Prozac. One minute he's all quiet and serious and wants to play Scrabble with Sam, and the next minute he walks in, acting like Mick Jagger, and dressed like Prince.'

'I know, darling, he's under a lot of pressure at work. People express it differently. I think dressing like that relieves some of the stress for him.'

'I'm not sure which way I like him better. I've kind of gotten used to him looking normal. This is a little embarrassing. Last time I thought it was cool, now I think it looks silly.' She was growing up, and I smiled at her.

'He'll get over it again in a couple of weeks, Char. I promise.'

'Whatever.' She shrugged and took the salad out to the table. Paul was already sitting there with Sam, and regaled all of us with outrageous stories of meetings he had disrupted with whoopee cushions and live frogs over the years. It was a side of him that Sam particularly loved, and I found myself staring at him. Like Charlotte, I had gotten used to Peter, and now seeing Paul again was a little confusing. I wasn't sure I was up to another two weeks of intense ecstasy and the quadruple flip. In my heart of hearts, I had come to love Peter's quieter ways better. And in his own way, he was twice as sexy as Paul. Paul took a lot of energy, and he consumed enough bourbon for the entire state of Nebraska. I didn't even have champagne in the house for him. He asked for dessert, but settled for half a bottle of Yquem that was still left over from the last time.

He taught Sam how to play poker that night, and played liar's dice with Charlotte after that, and after they had both beaten him, they went to bed, still amused at how he was behaving. He had told them that he decided not to go to California. He claimed he was staying with us because he had lent his apartment to friends from London. Paul was very considerate about explaining things to the kids, so they wouldn't know the truth about him, or that Peter was gone.

But once the kids were in bed, I was honest with him, and told him what I was thinking.

'Paul, I'm not sure you should stay here. Things have gotten serious with Peter in the last few months. I don't think he'd like it.' More importantly, I didn't think I would. This was just too confusing for me.

'This was his idea, Steph. I wouldn't be here if he hadn't sent me. I got the call from his office.' That surprised me. He hadn't seemed all that pleased about what happened when he sent the Klone in September. 'He expects us to be together while he's away.'

'Why? I can manage fine on my own for two weeks.' It made me seem like a nymphomaniac or something, as though I had to have sex fourteen times a day and hang off the chandelier while doing it, just because Peter was in California. And it wasn't that simple for me. Besides, I had plenty to do with the kids, getting ready for the holidays, I had started looking for a job, and I had lots of parties to go to. I tried to explain that to Paul, as we sat in the living room and he opened another bottle of bourbon.

'He probably doesn't want you going out alone at this time of year, Steph. He must have had a reason for calling me, and having me come to see you.'

'Maybe I should ask him,' I said, wondering how best to handle an awkward situation like this one.

'I wouldn't do that. I think he likes knowing I'm here, but I'm not sure he wants to hear about it.' I had figured that much out the last time. 'Kind of like an imaginary friend, if you know what I mean.' But I knew better.

'Paul, there is nothing imaginary about you. My back hurt for two months after you left.' The quadruple wasn't as simple as it looked, no matter how skilled he was at it. Peter was right. It was dangerous. And he'd sent me to his chiropractor, which had finally helped me. He hadn't asked how I'd hurt my back, but I was sure he knew without asking.

'Tell me about it. They had to replace all the wires in my neck after last time,' Paul said, and then he smiled at me so winningly I felt something in me start to melt, in spite of my good intentions, and my resistance to him. 'But it was worth it. Come on, Steph . . . for old times' sake . . . just two little weeks. It's Christmas. If I go back now, I'll feel like a failure.'

'It might be the best thing for both of us. What's the point of this? I'm in love with him, and you know it. I don't want to spoil it.'

'You can't. I'm his Klone, for heaven's sake. I'm him, and he's me.'

'Oh God, not that again,' I said, feeling overwhelmed by his persona. 'I can't go through this again.'

'Didn't you feel closer to him last time after I left?' he said, looking hurt that I doubted his good intentions.

'How did you know that?' The truth was, I had. But he had no way of knowing. Or did he?

'Steph, it's meant to. I think that's why he sent me. Maybe I show you a side of him he doesn't know how to show you himself.' I glanced at the chartreuse pants and the rhinestone-encrusted T-shirt as he said it, but I found his theory a little hard to swallow. There was so much to Peter as it was, if he had a side like this, I wasn't sure he needed to show it to me. This was just a crazy experiment someone had dreamed up, or Peter had, and it had gotten out of hand right from the beginning. It was an insane fantasy to live out, and I was convinced I didn't need to. It was his fantasy not mine, and I was no longer sure it was even Peter's. 'Look, let me spend the night,' he persisted in spite of all my rationalizations. 'No double flip, no triple, no quadruple. We'll just lie in bed and talk, like good friends, old times. And I'll leave in the morning, I promise.'

'Where will you go?'

'Back to the shop. To take my head off.' Poor thing. It was a rotten way to spend Christmas. We deserved a little fun at least before he went back in the shop again. After all, he had been there since September, waiting for Peter to leave for California.

'All right. But just tonight. And no funny stuff. You can wear a pair of his pajamas.'

'Do I have to? Christ, they're so ugly. They're probably beige or something.' He winced at the prospect, as though their oatmeal blandness would cause him genuine pain. He would have felt differently if they'd been chartreuse satin.

'They're navy, with red trim. You'll love them.'

'I doubt it. But for you, I'll wear them.' I was only sorry I had finally disposed of my very last flannel nightgown. They were gone forever. I had already decided to sleep in my bathrobe,

just to be safe. I didn't want to provoke Paul
into anything we'd both regret later.

We went to bed eventually, and used the
bathroom separately. He came out wearing the
navy blue pajamas, looking as though he might
get sick from wearing them, and I came out
wearing my most chaste nightgown, and the
terry-cloth bathrobe he had bought me at '21.'
It was a far cry from the last time I'd seen him.
And this time, there were no candles. Peter was
right, I had decided, they were a fire hazard.

'Not even one little one?' Paul looked
crushed when I told him. He loved candlelight,
and so did I now.

'No. I'm turning the light off,' I warned him,
and got into bed next to him, but as soon as he
put an arm around me, he felt just like Peter. I
had to keep reminding myself he wasn't, but it
was hard to remember in the dark.

'Why are you so uptight tonight?' he asked
unhappily, as I lay tensely next to him. 'He
must be making you frigid or something. No
wonder he had them send me.'

'You are not here on a mission,' I reminded
him. 'You're here to visit, as an old friend, and

a figment of his occasionally insane imagination.' For the past three months, Peter had seemed so normal, that it was hard to remind myself now that the Klone had originally been his idea and creation.

'What about your imagination, Steph? Have you lost it entirely, or has he killed it?'

'No, he has made me very happy.'

'I don't believe you,' he said firmly. And I frowned in the darkness. I didn't like the way the conversation was going. I hadn't invited him to stay so I could defend myself. I had let him stay because I felt sorry for him. 'If you were so happy, you'd still be as much fun as you used to be. Now you're more uptight than he is.'

'I can't sleep with both of you. It makes me crazy.'

'I am not "both of us." We are one person.'

'Then you're both nuts.'

'Possibly. But we also both love you.' He said it matter-of-factly.

'I love you too. I just don't want to confuse myself again. Last time, when I was with you, I thought I loved you and not him. Then when he came back, I knew I loved him, and not you. And by then, you had your head off anyway, so the whole thing was insane.' How could I ever discuss this with him? But he seemed to want to. And he looked irritated when he answered.

'You know where your head is, don't you?'

'Don't be insulting.'

'Why don't you just shut up for a minute,' he said, and before I could stop him, he kissed me. And in spite of all my stern resolve, it started all over again. I could suddenly feel everything I'd felt for him the last time, in spite of the promises I'd made myself not to.

'No!' I said, and then kissed him again, hating myself more than him. It was ridiculous. As soon as he touched me, I had absolutely no resistance, no morals.

'That's better,' he said, and kissed me again, and I wanted to hit him. But I didn't. I just went on kissing him, and after a while I didn't want to stop. I just wanted to lie there, kissing him forever. Until he touched me. And suddenly the kisses weren't enough, and I wanted all of him, and the worst part was that the whole time I kept missing Peter, and at the same time feeling Paul was part of him. It was impossible to sort out who was who and what was what, and whom I was doing what with, and why. And by the time it was all over, I was as crazy as they were, and I no longer cared which of them was in bed with me. I was happy and peaceful, and even the double flip seemed funny to me when we finally did it.

'You're terrific,' he said, as I lay thinking afterward, about what a strange gift this was, and how much they both meant to me, although I still preferred Peter to Paul, and knew I always would. But I also loved Paul's whimsy.

'I think you're bad for me,' I lied to him, wanting him to feel guilty, because I didn't. After all, this was all Peter's fault anyway. He had invented him, and sent him to me. If he hadn't wanted this to happen, he shouldn't have given him to me. But what if it was a test of some kind, of my chastity and fidelity? In that case, I had a serious problem, because as long as it was Peter's Klone I was sleeping with, and not some stranger, I didn't really care. For all intents and purposes, Paul appeared to be the same man, the same face, the same body, the same spirit. Only the wardrobe was different, and then there was the triple flip, which was even more different, and quite terrific.

'I am not bad for you,' Paul objected. 'Don't make this into something it isn't, and doesn't have to be.' It sounded like gibberish to me.

'Then what is this? You explain it to me. Because I can't,' I said, feeling confused by what he was saying, and I was feeling.

'It's a fantasy. An extension of him. Besides, I give great jewelry. Which reminds me.' With that, he turned the light on, dug into the pocket of Peter's pajamas lying on the floor, and pulled out an enormous diamond bracelet and handed it to me.

'Oh my God, what is that?'

'What does it look like? It's not a tennis racket, or a pet snake. I stopped off at Tiffany on my way over.'

'Oh Paul . . . you really are crazy . . . but I love it.' I grinned from ear to ear as he put it on me. 'Now I really should feel guilty. You're going to think you can just buy me.'

'I can't afford you. Only he can. Why don't

you just marry him, Steph, and get it over with, instead of all this back and forth between your apartments, and hiding from the kids. It's a stupid waste of time. Besides, you love each other.'

'That's beside the point.'

'No, it's not. That *is* the point,' he said wisely.

'I'm not sure what the point is. I was married, and after thirteen years, Roger said he had never loved me. I can't go through that again.'

'He's a jerk, and you know it. Peter isn't.'

'No, but in any case, he hasn't asked me. And what would happen to us, if he did? That would mean curtains for us. No more jewelry.'

'Don't be so greedy. Besides, it would be up to him. He might still want me to be with you when he goes to California.'

'I doubt it,' I said honestly, wondering just how crazy I was, having this conversation with a Klone, not even a real person. But he was smart, almost as smart as Peter in some ways, and in my own way I loved him, though not as much as I loved Peter. At times, Paul was adorable, at other times, he just seemed like a poor imitation of Peter.

'He'd probably take you to California with him,' Paul said thoughtfully. 'He would if he's smart, anyway. And if not, it's the quadruple flip for us forever. Worse things could happen to you. I think you really love him. Sometimes I think it's the only reason why you love me.' It was the truth, of course, but I hated to hurt his feelings. In some ways, Paul was so easily wounded. It was hard to remember he had wires instead of a heart.

'Anyway, I'm not going to marry him. So you're just going to have to keep buying me jewelry, and charging it to him forever. Get used to it.'

'The trouble is, I have,' he said gently, as we lay side by side, with his arm around me in the dark. I was glad he had come back by then, and I was beginning to realize how much I had missed him. He said things to me that Peter never would have. 'I'd really miss you,' he said sadly, 'if he didn't let me come back again.'

'Don't worry about it . . . let's get some sleep,' I said, yawning, and when he turned over on his side, I cuddled up next to him. There was something very vulnerable about him this time,

which really touched me deeply. And five
minutes later, he was sleeping soundly, as I lay
next to him, thinking about the things he had
said, and the things I was feeling. It was all so
damnably confusing. It was like sleeping with
two men, all rolled into one, and I was never
quite sure where one man ended and the other
began. It was the price I paid for sleeping with
a Klone, a man made up of computer chips and
wires. But there was more to Paul than met the
eyes. There was always the quadruple flip to
think about, and the jewelry. I smiled to myself
as I fell asleep cuddled up next to him, happy
that Peter had decided to send him.

Chapter Eight

For the next few days, I indulged myself totally. We did all the same things we had done before. We stayed in bed all day while the kids were at school. I postponed looking for a job till January. We did the triple flip all night, and he had a great time with the children on the weekend. We even took them skating at Rockefeller Center, and he wore a one-piece sky-blue spandex jumpsuit with rhinestones on the collar. It was fairly conservative for him, but he was a terrific skater, and everyone at the rink loved him.

He finally went to the office later one afternoon, to take care of some things for Peter. Peter had called several times from the West

Coast, and seemed to be having a lot of business problems. This time I didn't say a word about Paul, or the fact that he was with me again. I figured that he either knew, or didn't want to know, so I kept my own counsel. And Paul was keeping me very busy. But this time it was different.

I was feeling tortured by loving both of them, and even the gifts Paul showered me with made me uncomfortable, especially knowing he was charging them to Peter. But that day, when he left for work, I called the psychiatrist I had seen briefly when Roger left me. The doctor seemed surprised to hear from me. It had been almost two years since I'd seen him, and I guess he had assumed that I had either killed myself, gone back to Roger, or found someone new to torture myself with. I was lucky, he had just had a cancellation, and told me he could see me in half an hour, if I could be there promptly, which I promised I would.

His office hadn't changed much in two years, the couch I sat on, facing him, seemed a little more worn, and the pictures on the wall seemed a little more depressing. He had lost more hair, and the carpet looked threadbare. Other than that, the place looked terrific. And he seemed happy to see me. And after the initial amenities, I decided to get to the point. I was feeling utterly confused about Peter and Paul. I was more in love with Peter than ever. He was everything I had ever wanted, and we got on perfectly when he was there. But when he wasn't, I was locked in this mad affair with Paul, my imaginary friend, as he called himself now, but the trouble was, he wasn't. He got more real to me every day, and I had him under my skin again in a way that really scared me, which was why I had come to see Dr Steinfeld.

'So, Stephanie, what brings you here to see me?' Dr Steinfeld asked kindly. 'You haven't gone back to Roger, have you?'

'Oh God, no.' In fact, Charlotte had just told me that he and Helena were having a baby, and the funny thing was I didn't care at all. I had always thought that if that happened, it would unnerve me. But I was too busy doing the quadruple flip with Paul, and missing Peter in California to care about Roger and Helena's baby.

'No, it's something else.' I didn't want to waste even a second of my hour telling him about Helena and the baby. 'I'm involved with two men, and it's driving me crazy. No, not two really, one. More or less.' I suddenly realized that this was not going to be easy, as Dr Steinfeld looked at me with interest.

'You're involved with one man, or two? I'm not sure I'm reading you clearly.' Funny, I wasn't reading me clearly either. And he looked nearly as confused as I was.

'One real one. The other one is imaginary. Except that I have great sex with him. He only shows up when the real man is away. Actually, the real man sends him to me.' Dr Steinfeld was nodding, and staring at me with fascination. I had clearly become more interesting, and much more neurotic than he ever thought I could be.

'And how is your sex life with the . . . er . . . real one?'

'Terrific,' I said with quiet certainty, and he nodded.

'I'm delighted to hear it. And the second man

is only a fantasy? Which is it? You can tell me. I know you trust me.'

'It's actually both. I know this will sound crazy to you, Dr Steinfeld. But the second man, Paul, is really the Klone of the first one. His name is Peter.'

'You mean they look very similar? Are they twins?'

'No, I mean they're the same person. Paul is Peter's clone, more or less. Peter is in bionics, and he's done some very unusual experiments, and I really love him.' Tiny little beads of sweat appeared on Dr Steinfeld's forehead. Admittedly, this wasn't easy for either of us, and I was almost sorry I had come to see him.

'Tell me, Stephanie, have you been taking any medication? Self-medicating perhaps? You know, some drugs have serious side effects and can cause hallucinations.'

'I am *not* hallucinating. Paul is Peter's bionic clone, and Peter sent him to me when he went out of town. I slept with him for two weeks last fall and it's just started again. I feel completely crazy. Whoever I'm with is the one I'm most in love with . . . except I always love Peter. He's the real one.'

'Stephanie,' he said firmly then, 'do you hear voices sometimes? Even when you're not with them?'

'No, I do not hear voices, Doctor. I am sleeping with two men, and I don't know what to do about it.'

'Then that's clear. Are they both *real* men, Stephanie? I mean humans, like you and I?'

'No,' I said cautiously, 'one isn't. Paul is here right now, because Peter is away. He sent him to me.'

Dr Steinfeld quietly mopped his brow and continued to stare at me, while I wished myself anywhere on the planet but in his office.

'Is Paul in the room with us right now?' he asked carefully. 'Can you see him now?'

'Of course not.'

'That's good. Do you feel abandoned when Peter leaves you? Do you need to fill that void with someone else, perhaps even someone imagined?'

'No. I don't just make him up because I

feel rejected. Peter sends him to me.'

'How does he send him to you?' On a UFO maybe. By then he was obviously expecting something like that from me. It was hopeless.

'Paul arrives with about fifteen pieces of matched purple alligator luggage from Hermès. He has pretty eccentric taste in clothes too, but he's a lot of fun to be with.'

'What about Peter? What is he like?'

'Wonderful, conservative, smart, loving, he's great with my kids, and I'm crazy about him.'

'And what does he wear?'

'Blue jeans and button-down shirts, and gray flannels and a blazer.'

'Does that disappoint you? Do you fantasize about him being more like Paul?'

'No, I love him the way he is. He's actually sexier than Paul, without even trying. My knees go weak when I see him.' I smiled then, just thinking about it.

'That's nice, Stephanie. Very nice. And how do you feel about Paul?'

'I love him too. He loves to have a good time, and he's pretty badly behaved sometimes. But he loves my kids too, and he's very lovable, and amazingly good in bed. He does this thing where he does somersaults in the air, and then lands on the floor with me on top of him, and . . .' I could see that Dr Steinfeld was rapidly approaching a nervous breakdown, and I felt sorry for him.

'Somersaults in the air? Is this the imaginary one, or the real one?'

'He's not imaginary. He's a Klone. A bionic clone. He has wires. But he looks just like Peter.'

'What happens when Peter returns, does he disappear again, or do you still "see" him?'

'No. They take him back to the shop, check his wires and take his head off.'

There was sweat running down the sides of Dr Steinfeld's face by then, and he was frowning at me. I hadn't gone there to torture him, but to relieve myself, and it obviously wasn't working. For either of us.

'Stephanie, have you ever considered taking medication?'

'Like what? Prozac? I used to take Valium. You prescribed it for me.'

'Actually, I was thinking of something a little

stronger. Something a little more suited to your problem. Like Depakote perhaps. Have you ever heard of it? Have you been taking medication since I last saw you?'

'No, I haven't.'

'Have you been hospitalized recently?' he asked sympathetically, and I started to panic, thinking he was about to call Bellevue to have me checked in. But maybe I belonged there.

'No. And I know this sounds ridiculous, but it really is happening. I swear it.'

'I know you believe that. I'm sure they both seem very real to you.' I could see in his eyes that he was convinced that I had invented both of them, and was utterly crazy, which was true, but not to the degree he thought so. I hated Peter suddenly for unleashing this problem on me in the first place. 'Now, our hour is up, but I want you to fill this prescription for some medication. And I'm going to make time to see you tomorrow.'

'I don't have time. Paul and I are taking the children Christmas shopping.'

'I see,' he said, looking even more worried. 'Does Roger have custody of them?'

'No, I do.' But suddenly all I wanted to do was laugh when I looked at him. He was so dismayed by what I had told him. I just wish he could have seen Paul in silver or gold lamé, puce, or chartreuse, or hot pink or bright purple. The leopard jumpsuit would have done it too, or the orange velour lounging suit he had worn the night before at dinner. Dr Steinfeld would have loved him. He would have understood why I was so confused.

'Do you get headaches, Stephanie? Severe ones?'

'No, doctor, I don't,' I said, smiling at him. I stood up then and he looked intensely worried. 'I'm really sorry this is all so confusing.'

'We'll get it all sorted out soon. You'll feel much better on the medication. It will take a few weeks to take hold, so it's very important you start right away. I want you to call me tomorrow and make another appointment.'

'I'll do that,' I said, and practically ran out the door before he could commit me.

I hailed a cab and went home, and found Paul playing with the kids. He was already into his second bottle of bourbon, and all I could do was look at him and shake my head, just like Dr Steinfeld.

'Are you okay?' he asked a few minutes later, when he came to see what I was cooking for dinner.

'No, I hate you,' and at that exact moment, I meant it. 'I went to my old shrink this afternoon, and thanks to you and that lunatic who sent you here, I convinced him that I'm completely crazy.'

'Did you tell him you're not, we are?'

'I tried to. But I think he's right. I think it's contagious.'

'What did he tell you to do?' Paul asked with interest.

'Take medications for my hallucinations. I told him you were a Klone, and he asked me if you were in the room with me at that moment. Nice, huh?'

'Very. Believe me, if I'd been there, he would have known it.'

'No kidding.' He was wearing zebra velvet pants, and a black satin shirt open to the waist, with his peace sign. 'He could have heard you, not just seen you.' Paul gave me a look. He

heard something in my voice. I just wasn't in
the mood for Paul's antics. For the first time, I
was actually sick of the outrageous clothes he
wore, the way he drank, and picking myself up
off the floor after the double flip. I really missed
Peter.

And after dinner, when Peter called me, I
took the phone in the bathroom to talk in
private.

'How's it going?'

'Fine, thank you. I'm completely crazy.'

'Are the kids giving you a hard time?'

'No, you are. Both of you,' I said, and he
understood instantly what I was saying.

'Is he there again?' He sounded surprised,
and not very happy about it.

'As if you didn't know. Didn't you send him?'

'Not this time. I thought you'd be okay
without him since you were so busy.'

'So how did he get here?' For once, I wasn't
sure I believed him. It was all too much now.

'Honest, Steph. I'm not sure. But if he's
bugging you, just send him away. I'll have him
picked up tomorrow. They'll take him back to
the shop, and take his head off.'

'No,' I said much too quickly. 'He can stay until you come back.' In spite of all the craziness of his being there, I wanted him to stay, but I didn't want to admit it to Peter.

'Do you want him there?' he asked, sounding upset.

'I don't know what I want anymore. That's the problem.' That much was the truth.

'I see.'

'Oh, for chrissake, you sound like Dr Steinfeld.'

'Who's that?' It was the first time he had heard about him.

'A shrink who would have liked to have me committed today. This is all your fault. Why can't you just go away and let me miss you, like normal people? Instead you have to send a goddam Klone to take care of me, and drive me insane.' I was suddenly angry about it. It was all very upsetting. And it was all Peter's fault, no matter how much I loved him.

'I thought you'd like him.'

'I do.'

'Maybe too much so. Is that what you're saying?' He sounded nearly as upset as I did, and more than a little jealous.

'I don't know what I'm saying. Maybe we're both crazy.'

'I'll try to come home early.' He sounded genuinely worried.

'Maybe the three of us should just live together. And by the way, Helena is having a baby.'

'Is that what's really bothering you?'

'Maybe. No, I don't think so. But the kids are upset about it. They hate her. And the idea of a baby.'

'I'm sorry, Steph.'

'No, you're not.' Suddenly, I was crying, and I heard Paul in the next room, with the children. 'He's an alcoholic, for chrissake, and if I see those goddam zebra pants again, I'm going to have a nervous breakdown. Maybe I am anyway. How did this ever happen to me?' It was all his fault, and I wanted to hate him for it. But I didn't. I still loved him. And I knew my kids did too. Even Charlotte, though she would have hated to admit it. And Sam had been his loyal follower for months, more than ever since

Peter had come to his rescue when Roger flaked out on him on Halloween.

'It was just an experiment, that's all. Don't take it so seriously.' We both sounded like crazy people, but thank God Dr Steinfeld couldn't hear us.

'Don't take it seriously? He's living here, and I'm in love with you, and sometimes I can't even tell you apart. When he's in the shower he looks like you. And when he gets dressed, he looks like goddam Elvis Presley.'

'I know. I know . . . we tried straightening that out, but he wouldn't let us.' I suspected he didn't want to ask me how I knew what Paul looked like in the shower, but it was easy to guess what was happening between us, from everything else. Besides, I figured that, better than anyone, Peter knew Paul only too well.

'He thinks you should marry me. Can you imagine that? He's crazier than you are.' I was crying by then, and at Peter's end, there was a long silence. 'Don't worry. I told him neither of us was crazy enough to do that.'

'I'm glad to hear it,' was all he said finally, sounding just a fraction cool.

'So am I. Maybe I need to leave both of you for a while, and try to get sane again.' I was better off alone back in front of the TV watching reruns. I thought I had a real life with Roger before that, but even that blew up in my hands. Now look what I had. The bionic man, and Dr Frankenstein, the mad inventor. I was so upset, I just sat there and cried.

'The holidays are hard for everyone, Steph. You're just upset. Try to relax. I'll be home soon, and he'll be back in the shop. If you want me to, I can have him dismantled.'

'That's a terrible thing to do to him. Besides, I like him.' Which brought us right back to the beginning. I loved Peter, but I didn't want to lose Paul. It was an insane situation.

'Just take it easy. Get some sleep tonight. He's sleeping in the guest room, isn't he?'

'Yeah, sure.' You fool, I wanted to say to him. What do you think? He hadn't been built to sleep in anyone's guest room. 'I love you,' I said forlornly.

'I love you too. I'll call you in the morning.'

He hung up then, and that night it was the same story all over again. I couldn't resist him. Quadruple flips and fantastic sex, candlelight and massages, and scented oil, and when morning came, I was still awake, and so confused, I hated both of them. I wanted Peter to come home, and the Klone to stay, and never to see either of them again, and if I never did another double or triple flip again it would be too soon, and I never wanted another piece of jewelry. I wanted it all to stay, and go away, and as I fell asleep finally, I was dreaming of Peter. He was standing there, watching me, with an arm around Helena, while Paul just stood there wearing those damn zebra pants again, and laughed at me.

Chapter Nine

By the end of Paul's second week with me, I was more confused than ever, but in spite of that, we always seemed to have a good time together. We went to all the Christmas parties I was supposed to go to, and in spite of a few minor faux pas, he actually did very well. I tried to get him to let me pick his outfits, but of course that was too much to ask. He had bought a silver suit with Christmas balls hanging all over the jacket, and the trousers were covered with tiny colored lights. He thought it incredibly festive, and the hostess at the first party we went to thought it was an enchanting joke. Little did she know he meant it, and felt he had made the fashion statement of the season.

He devoured all the hors d'oeuvres, gobbled up all the caviar, and when they ran out, he put their tropical fish in his drink and swallowed them too. I don't think anyone noticed, but I did, and we left before he could get seriously out of hand or upset the hostess more than he already had.

The second party we went to was given by old friends of mine who had met Peter. They sang Christmas carols, had a fabulous buffet, and insisted on playing charades after dinner in the living room. I did *Gone With the Wind*, and no one guessed it, which must have sparked something for Paul. Because he chose a single word, a 'short one,' he gestured, and it only took me a few seconds to realize that the word he was acting out was *fart*. You can imagine what he did to get the point across. We left the party a little early that night, but in spite of my apologies, the host and hostess assured me that Paul had been a huge hit, particularly with their kids. They said he seemed a lot more 'outgoing' than the first time they'd met him, and was a true free spirit, and keeping a close eye on him, I agreed with them all the way out.

But I was furious with him for his outrageous behavior, and I said so in no uncertain terms after we'd left their apartment.

'That was a bit much, didn't you think?' I scolded him in the cab on the way home. I was not amused.

'What? The Christmas carols? No, I thought it was nice.'

'I mean what you did when you played charades. They were doing movies, Paul. I have never seen a movie called *Fart*.'

'Don't be so uptight, Steph. They loved it. Everyone laughed. It was so easy, I couldn't resist. It was their fault anyway. They shouldn't have served beans on the buffet. There's nothing Christmasy about beans,' he said matter-of-factly.

'No one forced you to eat them. You embarrassed me.' But as soon as I said it, he looked devastated.

'Are you mad at me, Steph?' But just looking at him in his Christmas ball suit, with the pants all lit up, I shook my head. How could I be? He was so lovable and so silly.

'I guess not, but I should be.' The worst of it

was that as irritating as he could be, I knew I would miss him as soon as he left. And that day was coming soon. We only had a few days left. There was something about him that always hooked me, and I knew it wasn't his wardrobe, or even the double flip. There was something so basically decent about him, so innocent and so loving. He was agonizingly hard to resist. And I couldn't.

'I love you, Steph,' he said, snuggling close to me in the cab. 'I wish I could spend Christmas with you.' I wanted to tell him I did not, but it wouldn't have been true. There were times when I wanted him to stay forever, with his crazy clothes and his outrageous behavior. He wasn't easy to take to parties, and yet when we were alone, we were always so happy.

He felt so remorseful about upsetting me that night that he suggested we stop at Elaine's for a drink. It had always been one of my favorite places with Roger, and I hadn't been there since he left me, but the idea appealed to me, and after hesitating for a minute, I agreed to go with him.

The cab dropped us off on the corner, and he

put his arm around me, as we walked toward
Elaine's. There was a huge, festive crowd at the
bar as usual, and Paul ordered a double
bourbon straight up and a glass of white wine
for me. I didn't really want it, but it felt good to
be there, and in spite of the ridiculous suit he
was wearing, I was happy to be with him. And
the crowd at Elaine's was eccentric enough that
I figured he could get by there without
attracting too much attention. It wasn't as difficult as going to a place like '21' with him.

But I had just taken the first sip of my wine,
when I turned and suddenly found myself
staring at Helena in a red velvet cocktail dress
trimmed in white rabbit or some kind of fur that
was shedding in white clouds all over everyone
standing at the bar near her. But far more
impressive than the fur she was shedding was
the amount of cleavage the dress left exposed.
All I could do was stare at her enormous white
bosom, it was so impressive it distracted one
completely from noticing her ever so slightly
protruding belly. And as I looked up I saw
Roger, watching me watch her, and looking
desperately uncomfortable, and then he

glanced at Paul. The balls on his Christmas
jacket suddenly looked larger than ever, and
even in the crowd at the bar, the lights on his
pants seemed to surround him in a kind of
glow.

'What is that?' Roger said without preamble,
staring at him in amazement. He knew about
Peter from the kids, but nothing they had said
had prepared him for what he saw.

'That's Paul . . . I mean Peter,' I said calmly,
brushing some of the fur Helena's dress had
lost off my nose.

'That's quite an outfit,' Roger said express-
ively, which Paul took as a compliment, but I
knew Roger better, and saw with ease that he
was appalled. 'Thank you. It's Moschino,' he
explained pleasantly, with no idea who Roger
was, much less Helena. 'I usually wear Versace,
but I couldn't resist this for the holidays. What
kind of fur is that?' he asked, staring at Helena's
cleavage, and then turned to me with a smile.
'Friends of yours?'

'My ex-husband, and his wife,' I said tersely,
and then turned to my successor. I had to be
polite for the children's sake, or maybe for

Roger's. 'Hello, Helena.' She gave me a nervous smile, and then told Roger she was going to powder her nose. She disappeared into the crowd in a cloud of white fur, as Roger grinned at the man he thought was Peter. He would have really had a rough time with it if he knew Paul was a Klone.

'The children have told me about you,' Roger said vaguely, as Paul nodded, and then told me he was going to see about getting us a table, and the next thing I knew Roger and I were alone, for the first time in ages. 'I can't believe you'd go out with a guy who looks like that,' he said bluntly.

'At least I didn't marry little Miss Santa. I thought you were allergic to fur.' Or maybe he was just allergic to my flannel nightgowns and the fur on my legs.

'That's uncalled for,' he said bluntly. 'She's the mother of your children's half-brother or -sister,' he said coldly, looking just like the man I had come to hate in the end.

'Being married to you and getting pregnant doesn't make her respectable, Roger. It just makes her as dumb as I was. For now at least.

What do you two talk about anyway, or do you bother to talk to her at all?'

'What do you do with him in that suit? Sing "Deck the Halls"?'

'He's nice to our kids. That counts for a lot,' and it was more than I could say for Helena, but I didn't say it to him. There was no point, but the children still reported every time they saw them that she never even talked to them, and she could hardly wait for them to leave on Sunday afternoon. I knew Roger had to know it too, and I wondered how he felt about it, and how much worse it would get after their own baby was born. But that was another matter, and not something that could be resolved at Elaine's. I was sorry we had come there, and had seen them. Roger didn't look any better than he had when he left me two years before. In fact, he looked a lot more tired, and a little older, and extremely bored. Helena was no brain-trust, but I had to admit she was striking and sexy, and her cleavage was pretty impressive, whether or not it was draped in rabbit fur. It wasn't too obvious yet that she was pregnant, but I suspected her boobs had grown even larger than the last time I'd seen them.

'Are you okay?' he asked suddenly, with a wistful look, and I hated him for it. I didn't want him to be human, and more than anything I didn't want him to feel sorry for me because I was out with a Klone covered in blinking lights and Christmas balls.

'I'm fine, Roger,' I said quietly. But as I said it, I wasn't so sure that I was. I was in love with a most unusual man who was in California doing odd scientific things I didn't understand, and who had no desire to get married, and in his absence, I was sleeping with his Klone. It was not only tough to explain to Roger, but a little hard to come to terms with myself. As I thought about it, Paul returned from wherever he had been.

'We got a table,' he said proudly, reaching for my glass of wine, but all I wanted to do was go home. I could see Helena approaching, preceded by a small cloud of flying fur.

'It was nice to see you,' I said to Roger politely. 'Merry Christmas,' and with that, I set down my wine, and left the bar with Paul. We passed Helena on the way, and I could smell her perfume. It was one I had worn ten years before, and I knew Roger had bought it for her, because it was one he really loved. He was hers now, and they had their own life. They were having a baby, and whatever mess I had made with my own life, it was not his problem, and maybe not even Peter's or Paul's.

I told Paul that I wanted to leave then, and he looked disappointed about the table, but he could see in my eyes that something was wrong. He followed me outside, and looked at me in the freezing night air as I took a deep breath, as much to free myself of the familiar sight and scent of Roger as of Helena's perfume and her fur.

'What happened?'

'I don't know,' I said, shaking in the December air, it had just started to snow. 'I didn't expect to see them . . . she's such a bimbo, and he's crazy about her. It was like a reminder of everything I felt when he left me. He left me for her.' I felt vulnerable and naked, and the cheesy dress and brassy hair were no consolation. The truth was he hadn't loved me. And for now at least, he loved her. I didn't want him anymore, that wasn't the point, and I wouldn't have taken him back if he'd asked me, but it still rubbed all my broken dreams in my face again.

'Don't feel bad, Steph,' Paul said kindly. 'She's a giant zero. Her boobs aren't even real . . . and Christ, that awful dress! You're ten times better-looking than she is. Believe me. And who wants a woman with that kind of taste?' As he said it, his pants were twinkling brightly, and the Christmas balls on his jacket were dancing in the breeze, but somehow the look in his eyes touched me deeply, and he put one arm around me, hailed a cab with the other, and as we got into the taxi, he gently wiped away my tears.

'Forget them. We'll go home and light some candles, and I'll give you a massage.' And for once, it sounded like just what the doctor ordered. I was quiet in the cab, still shaken by the encounter, and Paul was gentle and understanding when we went upstairs.

I paid the sitter and was relieved to find that both kids had gone to bed early and were asleep. And that night, it was surprisingly soothing to let Paul massage me and eventually to let myself be transported by his gentle passion, and a very modest double flip.

I felt closer to Paul after that, he had gotten me through a tough moment, seeing Roger with Helena, and had restored a little of my self-esteem. We went to see the *Nutcracker* with the children that week. Paul went dressed as Turkish Coffee. He did an exotic dance in the aisle and tried to get me to do it with him. And then we took Sam to see Santa, and Paul sat on Santa's lap after Sam did. He also picked out beautiful gifts for both Charlotte and Sam. In his own way, he did a lot of things right. And being with him reminded me of all the things Peter wasn't. It was as though someone had programmed Paul to do all the things Peter didn't do for me. The gifts, the time he spent with me, his childlike spirit when he played with Charlotte and Sam. The endless tenderness he showed me. He was impossible to resist, harder still not to love. And beneath all the absurdities and inappropriate behavior, he was a very good man. Or should I say, good Klone. Peter had done an extraordinarily fine job when he designed him.

Peter was calling me from California two and three times a day. And he couldn't help asking about Paul. He wanted to know what we were doing, what Paul was saying, what he was charging to him, and if he was driving the Jaguar. I wasn't going to tell him that he was, but in the end I had to, when he had another accident with it on the FDR Drive. It was snowing that afternoon, and the road was icy. And when he told me about it, I was just glad I had forbidden the children to go in the car with him. He had been singing to himself and listening to Peter's CD's, most of which he hated, but he liked the Whitney Houston CD I'd given him, and while he was singing, he sneezed apparently, and drove the car right off the road and onto the snow piled to one side. The car sat poised there for an interminable instant, while Whitney kept singing, and then it slid slowly down the other side and into the shallow water at the edge of the East River. It sat there half-submerged while Paul waited for the AAA for nearly two hours. He said it had been rough on the upholstery and the rugs were soaked when they finally pulled it out. He was afraid it might need a new engine, and hoped that Peter wouldn't mind too much.

I called Peter and told him, and he just groaned, and then whimpered pitifully when I told him what it would cost him to repair it.

'Just don't let him repaint it again,' was all Peter said before he hung up.

'How was he?' Paul asked, looking worried, when I told him what Peter had said about the Jaguar.

'Cranky,' I explained, but I was worried about Paul. After his little dip in the East River, he was catching a terrible cold. 'He'll be all right,' I said gently. And then I told him the bad news. 'He's coming back tomorrow.'

'So soon? That's two days early.' Paul looked crushed. He'd been planning to spend the rest of the week with me, before Peter got back from California.

'He says he has a board meeting he has to be at.' But I suspected it was more than that, and not just the car either, I had the feeling that he didn't want Paul staying with me anymore. And I could see Paul was upset about it.

We spent a quiet night that night, I wrapped him in blankets for his cold, and served him hot toddies, and every time I kissed him he sneezed, and his nose was red. But as sick as he was about to be, I knew the Jaguar looked much worse. And then, as I climbed into bed with him, he turned to me with an unusually serious air. He looked as though he had a lot on his mind, and he seemed uncharacteristically unhappy.

'What would happen if I stayed here?' he asked, looking worried, and I smiled. Maybe he had hit his head in the Jaguar.

'I seem to recall that you are, or have you forgotten?' I kissed him gently and he set down his glass on the table next to the bed, and then looked at me with concern.

'I mean after Peter gets back. What would happen if we told him I'm staying, and I'm not going back to the shop?' It was the first time he had ever said anything like that.

'Could you do that? Would they let you?' Just looking at the tenderness in his eyes, I was stunned, and a little worried.

'I could try. I can't leave you, Steph. I belong

here. I love you . . . we're happy together. You need me.' I did, more than I had ever planned to, maybe even more than I could admit, but the truth was that I needed Peter too, far more than I loved or needed Paul. I had gotten caught up in the good times we had again, but in the last few days, I had thought a lot about Peter coming home. Peter was the one embedded deep in my heart. Paul was the fun, the life, the spirit, the laughter. But Peter owned a piece of my soul. I had just come to understand that lately. I needed more in my life than a quadruple flip, and a good time. I needed Peter's solidity, his strength, his quieter style to shore me up and feed the parts of me that Roger had starved for so long, possibly forever.

'I don't know what to say,' I said honestly as we lay there. 'I love you, Paul.' And then I realized I had to be honest with him. 'But maybe not enough. We'd have a lot to overcome. It's not easy being with a Klone. We'd be shunned by society if people ever found out. It could get very rough.' It was true, and we both knew it. I had thought about it a lot. And it wasn't that his offer wasn't tempting. There was no doubt about it, it was. But with Peter, if he'd ever let me, I could have a real life. With Paul, I knew I couldn't.

'I'd marry you, Steph,' he said in a gentle whisper, and just hearing those words meant a lot. 'He won't.' I sensed as Paul did that Peter had gotten too used to being on his own. Although I knew he loved me, his fear of commitment was in fact more powerful than his love.

'I know,' I said quietly. 'But I love him anyway. I'm not even sure that matters to me anymore. I've been there, I've done that, I was married to Roger, and it all went wrong anyway. Marriage isn't a guarantee,' I said wisely, I knew whereof I spoke, better than Paul, 'all it is is a promise, an act of faith, a symbol of hope.' That was a lot, I had to admit, but I also knew it wasn't a fair trade. There was always one who loved, and one who walked, sooner or later.

'It's what you want. You'll never get that from him. If he had to make a choice, he'd rather have you marry me. Do you think if he really loved you, he'd put up with me staying here every time he goes away, massaging you, and loving you, and taking you out to parties and dinners, and teaching you the double flip? Or even the quadruple?'

'Maybe not,' I said sadly. 'But that doesn't change how I feel about him.'

'You were a fool once with Roger. Don't be a fool twice.' He was begging me and I couldn't bear to look at him.

'It could be too late for that,' I admitted. 'I already am a fool about him.'

'We could have a great life, Steph, if you were willing to try it.' But the truth was, I wasn't. Much as I loved him, I couldn't entrust my life to a Klone, not entirely, no matter how alluring he was, or how much fun. There was still a lot he was not. I couldn't spend the rest of my life with a man who played charades and enacted the word *fart* at a dinner party. 'You're missing the opportunity of a lifetime, Steph. You'd be the envy of all your friends.'

'I already am,' I said gently. 'You're the best,' and then I sighed, and decided to tell him the truth. 'I think I'm going to leave him, Paul,' I said sadly, tears already filling my eyes, and as he saw them, Paul looked shocked. He handed me a Kleenex and blew his nose too. He cried easily, which I knew was only a flaw in one of his wires, but it still touched me.

'When?' he asked.

'Soon. Probably after the holidays.' I had been thinking of it for days but I hadn't wanted to say anything to him. I thought I should tell Peter first. It seemed only fair. But it had implications for Paul too. It meant he wouldn't be coming back to see me anymore. How could he? If I gave up Peter, I would inevitably lose Paul. It was a rough decision to make, and I hadn't entirely made up my mind yet. But I knew I was much too in love with Peter, and far too entranced with Paul. They were both somewhat addictive, particularly in tandem. But the situation was just too insane. I couldn't go on sleeping with both of them. And as much as I loved Peter, I knew it was wrong. I couldn't go on being with him, and then living with Paul every time he left. Even if they had no qualms about it, I did. And I had my children to think of too. It had gotten too crazy this time. I was just too confused.

'Steph, are you sure?'

'Of course not,' I said, as fresh tears rolled down my face. 'How can I leave him? He's wonderful, and I love him so much.' More than I could ever say. But what was the point of going on like this? I couldn't face the future watching him come and go, driving myself crazy over what could never be, and then consoling myself with Paul. Even if he didn't understand how wrong it was, I did. After all, although I wouldn't have said it to him quite so bluntly, he was only a Klone. And Peter was only a man. And this whole harebrained scheme had been his idea. It obviously suited him, and took a lot of the pressure off for him. He could be with me while he was in New York, whenever he wanted, and whenever he wanted to get away, there was always Paul. It was the perfect arrangement for him. It would have almost been easier to live with his trips to California, no matter how frequent they were, and be alone with my kids.

'Don't do anything hasty, Steph,' Paul urged me as we both started getting sleepy. 'If you give him up, you lose me too.'

'I know.' It was a sobering thought, and I still had more thinking to do about it.

We tried the quadruple that night, after I stopped crying, and it went pretty well, although afterward I wondered if I might have cracked one of my ribs. I didn't want to upset Paul, so I didn't tell him, but as I lay in bed next to him afterward, thinking, he took my left hand and I felt him slip a ring on my finger.

'What are you doing?' I asked, looking worried, but he couldn't see the look on my face in the dark. I was hoping it was something he had found in a Cracker Jack box somewhere, but knowing him, that seemed unlikely. I finally couldn't stand the suspense anymore, turned on the light, and looked.

I gasped when I saw it. It was the most exquisite ruby ring I had ever seen, nearly forty carats, in the shape of a heart.

'Paul, you can't do this . . . I won't let you . . . this time it really is too much.' And I honestly meant it.

'It's all right, Steph,' he said smiling. 'I charged it to him.' I was sure he had, but even so, it was an incredible gift, and a spectacular ring. But I wondered what the implications of it were, and I looked at him with a question in my eyes. But Paul smiled at me and shook his head. 'It's not an engagement ring. It's a Christmas present . . . to remember me by.' There were tears in his eyes as he said the words, and in mine as I kissed him.

'I love you, Paul,' I said, and meant it. For that moment in time, I didn't give a damn if he was only a Klone. He was the kindest, funniest, sweetest, sexiest man I had ever known. Maybe even more than Peter.

'I love you too, Steph. I want you to take care of yourself while I'm gone. Don't let him drive you crazy . . . or break your heart. He will if you're not careful.' He already had in a way, but I didn't want to face it.

'He does anyway, drive me crazy, I mean. And so do you.' But the rewards he gave me almost made it worth it, I thought as I looked down at the enormous ruby heart. 'That's the trouble with all this,' I said, thinking out loud, as he looked at me.

'What? The jewelry?'

'No, the fact that you both drive me crazy.

Or maybe I already was. Maybe that's why he picked me. I guess he knew what he was doing in Paris.' But Paul knew, without even saying it to me, that Peter knew a lot of things. He was a smart man. The only thing he didn't know was if he really loved me. If he did, why would he want to share me with a Klone? There was more than just convenience involved, or the desire to show off an invention that was unique. I wondered if he wanted to get rid of me after all, if he *wanted* me to marry Paul. But whatever his intentions, or his twisted theories, I knew that I loved Peter, and only to a lesser degree, Paul.

And musing over all of it for the hundred millionth time, I put my arms around Paul with the ruby ring still on my finger, and fell asleep, but it was Peter I dreamed about all night as I slept fitfully till morning, not Paul, which told me something.

Chapter Ten

Given everything we'd said to each other the night before, it was very emotional for both of us when Paul left this time. There was no longer the absolute certainty that he would return. I couldn't promise him anything, and he knew it.

'In a few hours, I'll have my head off again, and all my wires hanging out, and you'll be back with him,' he said, looking mournful. 'I hate to think about it,' and then he looked at me with greater tenderness than I'd ever seen. 'I just want you to be happy, Steph. That's all. Do whatever you have to do.' And I knew, as I looked at him, that he meant it, and I loved him for it.

'Can I still see you if I leave him?' I was

worried now about all the things that I'd said. I wasn't feeling quite as brave, and worse yet when he shook his head, and almost started crying.

'No, you can't. It doesn't work like that. I can only stand in for him. I can't see you on my own.'

'But you said . . . you asked me to marry you last night . . .' I was confused. Would Peter have been part of it too? What was Paul thinking?

'I was kidding myself, Steph. We could get married, but I'd still be dependent on me.' He said it honestly, he didn't want to lie to her, he never had before and he wasn't going to start now. 'I'd have to share you with him, even if you loved me more.'

'Sometimes I think I do.' I was always honest too. But most of the time, I knew just how much I loved Peter.

'I think you're really in love with him Steph. Maybe you should explain that to him.'

'I'd probably scare him to death,' I said, looking pensive. And what was the point? Our relationship worked perfectly as it was. For him. Why ask for more? Why push it till it broke? I didn't want that.

'As Charlotte says, he's a dork,' Paul editorialized. 'Maybe you both are. It could just be you deserve each other. Life is too short to waste what you've got. Or even waste me. It drives me crazy to think I'm going to sit around now, for months, with my head off, while the two of you screw everything up. Just get him to work on his triple flip. But he's a real klutz. He could hurt himself. Be careful.' Paul was trying to cover how emotional he felt about leaving me, and I was especially worried about him when he showed up in black suede leggings with a black sequined jacket and high-heeled black alligator boots. I had never seen him looking so conservative or so somber.

'I don't like leaving you like this, Steph,' he said sadly, 'not knowing when I'll see you again, if ever.'

'I suspect you will.' I smiled sheepishly at him. How could you leave a man who had a Klone? Especially one like Paul. 'I'm not sure I could ever give either of you up. I think I'm hooked. I may have to go back to Dr Steinfeld again, to work things out, and that could take forever.'

'Please don't. You don't need him. You know what you want.' He smiled sadly at me, and I could see how much he loved me.

'Take care of yourself,' I said to him as he kissed me for the last time. I was still wearing his ruby ring and knew I always would. He said he wanted me to keep it.

'Give the kids my love.' They had already left for school. And then, he looked over his shoulder, as the elevator man piled all his luggage into the elevator, and said, 'Be happy, Steph, whatever you do.' The door closed behind him before I could answer, and I wondered if I would ever see him again. At that exact moment, I wasn't sure, and I already missed him.

And as I drove to the airport in a rented car, a frosted purple Tornado chosen by Paul, I could still hear the echo of Paul's words. I wondered where he was now, if his head was already off by then, if his wires were being pulled. I knew he had a couple of problems again. He had been smoking all week, from his left ear and right nostril, and I wasn't sure what that meant.

And as I stood at the gate, waiting for Peter, all I could think about was Paul. It was the most confusing relationship I'd ever been in. Roger had at least been boring. He slept a lot, and watched a lot of TV. He even watched *Jeopardy!* from time to time, and *Geraldo*, although he never admitted it when I walked into the room, and he clicked the set off. But there was nothing boring about Peter or Paul. Worse yet, they somehow complemented each other. Together, they were a whole man. And what a man!

I was still lost in my own thoughts as Peter walked off the plane, and I didn't even see him until he was standing next to me and pulled me into his arms without a word. He kissed me and then pulled away to look at me more closely.

'Are you okay?' he asked, looking me over carefully, as though he expected me to be different, but I was still the same, and just as in love with him as I had been since the summer. He was wearing a blazer and gray slacks and a gray turtleneck sweater, and a new pair of Gucci shoes he had bought in California. He looked as handsome as ever. He'd had a haircut while he was gone, and he looked sexy and powerful. 'I've been worried about you.'

'I've been fine.' I had been, except for my back, of course, after two weeks of the triple flip and the occasional quadruple. Paul had suggested I look into either a trainer, or a brace. 'How was California?'

'The same.' He told me about his trip as he went to pick up his luggage, and much to my surprise, he never asked me once about Paul. But as we headed for the garage, he noticed the heart-shaped ruby ring on my finger. 'Where did you get that?' he asked, looking worried. But I knew he suspected where it came from. And who was paying for it.

'From you,' I said quietly and he was polite enough not to comment. But he frowned and then groaned when he saw the purple Tornado.

'Did you have to rent a car that color?'

'It was all they had left,' I explained politely.

'How long will the Jaguar be in the shop?'

'Three months.'

'He's not having it repainted, is he?'

I hesitated for a fraction of a second and then

nodded. 'It's a lovely shade of periwinkle blue. Paul thought you'd love it.'

'Why not orange or lime green?' he said irritably, tossing his bags in the trunk and glaring at me.

'He thought you'd prefer the blue.'

'I'd prefer it if he didn't drive it when he visits. In fact,' he looked at me unhappily as he slipped behind the wheel, 'I think I'd prefer it if he didn't visit you. He just causes a hell of a lot of trouble, and he's a bad influence on the kids.'

'That's up to you,' I said meekly. I had never seen Peter in such a bad mood. It must have been a rough trip, or maybe he was just upset about the Jaguar.

'Yes, it is up to me,' he said sternly.

He didn't relax until we got home and I offered to massage him. He said his neck had been bothering him all week. It was obviously tension. But I'd had my fair share of that too. Bouncing back and forth between the two of them like a Ping-Pong ball wasn't exactly easy for me. And by that night, I was utterly confused again. I was beginning to feel as

though I needed an exorcist more than a
boyfriend. It was as though Peter had never
left at all and Paul had never existed. It was
eerie. I was in love with whichever one I was
with and always slightly less enamoured with
the other. At that moment, I was once again
profoundly entranced by Peter. He made
omelettes for me and the children, and acted as
though he'd never left us. The children no
longer even looked surprised to see him in gray
flannel instead of chartreuse. They had seen
him make that switch before, and still blamed
it on stress and mood swings, or trouble at the
office.

And after they went to bed, we wound up in
my bedroom, predictably, and he looked at me
with longing. I knew what he had in mind, and
I had the same intentions, but I warned him
that I wasn't up to the double flip. He looked
upset when I said it, and walked into the bathroom without saying a word. It was as though
he didn't like hearing about Paul anymore,
although it was Peter who had sent him.

I heard Peter take a shower, and he came
out in his navy pajamas, which I had washed

that morning, and the cleaning lady had pressed with infinite precision.

I had locked the door, and we were very quiet, so the children wouldn't hear, and it was only after we had made love, that he started to unwind. He put an arm around me, sighed deeply, and told me how much he had missed me. And just as it had been before, I knew with utter certainty that my heart was his and not Paul's. It was always so much fun being with Paul, but my relationship with Peter was more powerful and had deeper meaning.

But the transition still wasn't easy for me, and when he left at three o'clock that morning, all I could think of was Peter and not Paul. Being with Peter just seemed so much more real to me. But the odd thing was I was afraid that it was Paul who really loved me, and not Peter.

'I'll call you in the morning,' Peter whispered before he left, and I was sound asleep before he closed the door, dreaming of both of them, as they each held a hand out to me, and I wasn't sure which one to reach for.

And when I awoke the next morning, the sun was streaming into the room, but I felt a certain

sadness. It was odd not waking up and seeing
Paul. And I didn't know why, but I felt as
though sometime during the night, I had lost
him.

Peter said that I seemed quiet when he came
by at lunchtime, but I told him I was fine. I
had just been thinking of some of the things
that Paul had said. But more than ever, I was
aware of how difficult it all was, changing back
and forth from one to the other. Being so comfortable with Peter, and then having to adjust
to Paul. Getting used to all his tricks and
pranks, and wardrobe, spending my nights
doing triple flips, and then letting him go.
Back to Peter again. From love to lust and
back again to the point of madness. As much
as I loved this man, it was asking a lot to
expect me to love both man and Klone. And I
didn't want to say anything to Peter about how
difficult it was. But I suspect he knew it. I didn't
want to hurt his feelings, and it all sounded so
absurd. I didn't know anymore how long I
could continue. The only thing I did know was
how much Peter meant to me, what a rare gift
he was in my life. I knew that was a turning

point for me, but I didn't think he was ready to hear it.

'You miss him, don't you?' Peter asked when we went for a walk in Central Park that afternoon. It was snowing, and very cold. And I looked at him and nodded. I did. But he was, after all, only a Klone. I knew that now, a conglomeration of computer chips and wires enclosed in fuchsia satin. Peter had a mind, a heart, a soul, and much quieter taste in clothes. But in spite of that, I really loved him. 'I thought about it on the way home,' Peter said quietly. 'I haven't been very fair to you, have I?' He hadn't. But then again, what man was? Roger hadn't been fair either. And Peter seemed fairer than most. He was more of everything than any man I'd ever known. And he had a Klone, which made him doubly entertaining.

'I'm not complaining.' But I had to Paul. I had complained a lot about Peter's insensitivity to the situation, and my feelings.

'What does the ring mean? Just another gift, or something more?' He actually looked worried, as snowflakes settled on his hair and nose. He had stopped walking and was looking at me, with eyes full of questions. He looked tortured.

'Just another gift,' I said, looking pensive, remembering when Paul had put it on my finger. I hadn't taken it off since then.

'Did he propose?' I hesitated for a long time before I answered, not sure what Paul would want me to tell him. But my real loyalty was to Peter, and not to the Klone. I nodded silently as we walked.

'I thought so. And what did you say?' He looked grim, but as though he thought he had a right to know.

'I told him I couldn't marry a Klone,' I said simply.

'Why not?' Peter stopped walking again and looked at me as the snow fell all around us.

'You know as well as I do. I can't marry a Klone. He's a computer, a machine, a creation, not a human. It's ridiculous to talk about it.' Besides, and perhaps more importantly, I loved Peter, and not in any real sense Paul. No matter how appealing he was, Paul was merely an illusion. Peter was whole, or at least I thought so.

Peter was strangely quiet as we walked home. He said he had to go back to his apartment then, and he'd call me later. But by dinnertime, he hadn't called. The kids were with Roger for the rest of the weekend, and I called Peter several times that evening, but he never answered. I left him several messages, and then sat in the dark, in my bedroom, watching the snow, wondering where he was, and what had happened between us.

I didn't hear from him again until the next morning, and when he called, he sounded oddly cold. He said he'd had a call from California, and he was leaving that morning. He didn't want me to take him to the airport, and he'd be back in a few days. 'Before Christmas,' he said vaguely.

'Is something wrong?' The tone of his voice frightened me. He seemed suddenly very distant.

'No, it's just an emergency meeting. Nothing crucial, but I want to be there.' He offered no further explanation.

'I mean with us.' My voice was trembling as I asked. I had never heard him sound so cold.

He sounded like a different person.

'Maybe. We'll talk about it when I get home.'

'I don't want to wait that long.' I could hear it in his voice. The end had come. I suspected he wouldn't even bother to send Paul. Peter sounded as though he were retreating into his own world, and there was no room for me in it.

'I just need some time off,' he explained, but his voice sounded icy, as the snow continued to fall beyond the windows. 'I'll see you in a few days. Don't worry if I don't call.' I told him I wouldn't, and was crying when I set the phone down. Maybe it was another woman. Maybe that was why he was going back to California. Maybe this time he, instead of Paul, had been recalled, by a blonde in San Francisco. Another Helena. I was deeply worried about it.

I sat alone in the apartment that afternoon, turning it all over in my mind, wondering what had gone wrong, what I had done, why he seemed so cold and angry. We had been together for exactly five months by then, which seemed like a healthy chunk of time to me, but in the perspective of a lifetime was but a moment. I wondered if I'd hear from him at all, or if he'd even come back for Christmas as he'd promised. And his 'We'll talk about it when I get home,' sounded anything but happy. He said he'd call when he got back, and then hung up, without telling me he loved me. I could smell another heartbreak in my future. Perhaps even by Christmas, if I was very unlucky.

The children were due back at five-thirty, and half an hour before that, the doorbell rang. I figured Roger was dropping them off early, and went to open the door, still looking glum. I was very depressed about Peter. And as I pulled open the door, I saw Paul standing there, shaking the snow off his mink coat. He was wearing it over red spandex leggings and a shimmering red Versace sweater, with red alligator cowboy boots. Peter had sent him after all. For a moment I was relieved. At least I wouldn't be alone now.

'Hi,' I said glumly, as he swept me into his arms and off the floor, and spun me round till I was dizzy. He had on silver mittens with little ermine tails on them, and as he hugged me, he pulled them off and dropped them at my feet like gauntlets. I noticed then for the first time that he had new luggage. The purple alligator Hermès had disappeared, and he had bright red ostrich cases, made by Vuitton, with P.K. emblazoned on them in tiny pave diamonds.

'You don't look happy to see me,' he said, taking his coat off and looking disappointed. The truth was, I wasn't. I just couldn't play the game anymore. I had said my good-byes to him two days before, made my peace with it, knowing it might be the last time we would see each other. And then my heart had turned to Peter. He was all I could think of now, as I looked at Paul, desperately sorry this time that Peter had sent him to me.

'He left,' I said sadly, as twin tears rolled down my cheeks, longing for one of my old flannel nightgowns. I was in no mood for fun, or Paul. It was just too much for me to handle. I felt as though I were living in a revolving door, ricocheting from one to the other. But I knew where my heart had stopped now, and I knew better yet that Peter didn't care, and Paul was unable, or unwilling, to understand it. But at least, for once, I did.

'I know why you're upset,' Paul said happily,

grinning as he marched into the kitchen, track-
ing snow all over my front hall with complete
abandon. He opened the cupboard where the
bourbon was, and this time pulled out a bottle
of vodka. And within seconds had tossed down
two shots, and poured himself a third one. It
was the first time I'd ever seen him drink vodka,
but he seemed to love it. 'Peter said you were
missing me terribly,' he explained, looking
pleased with himself, and tenderly at me, 'that's
why he sent me.' He was strolling around my
kitchen, looking as though he owned it, which
annoyed me severely. He was, after all, only a
Klone, and he didn't own me.

'I wish he hadn't sent you, Paul,' I said
honestly. 'I'm not up to it. I don't think you
should stay,' I said sadly.

'Don't be silly.' He ignored me, as he
sprawled across a chair, and tossed back
another shot of vodka. 'He's not good for you
Steph. I think he depresses you. It must be the
way he dresses.' All I could think of was that
Paul looked like a giant strawberry as he sat
there in my kitchen in his red spandex leggings.
They were blinding.

'I *like* the way Peter dresses,' I defended him, and meant it. 'He looks wonderful and virile and sexy.'

'You think gray flannel is sexy?' I nodded and he groaned, licking his lips after the vodka. 'No, Stephanie, gray flannel is *not* sexy. It's boring.' He looked completely confident as he said it.

'I love him,' I said from across the room, watching him, wondering why I had ever thought I loved him. Paul was a cartoon, not a person. Actually, he was neither, but we both knew that. It didn't seem to daunt him.

'No, you don't Steph. You love me, and you know it.'

'I love being with you. I have fun with you. You're wild and funny and sweet and entertaining.'

'And great in bed,' he added, feeling the glow of the vodka. 'Don't forget that.'

'You don't have to do acrobatic acts to be great in bed,' I said quietly, I had never wanted to be in the circus.

'Stop making excuses for him. We both know the score. He's pathetic.'

'No,' I said, growing angry suddenly, 'you are. You think that you can just swoop in here whenever he leaves and play with me, flip me round in midair, drinking yourself blind, and make a fool out of me with my friends, and I'll be so blown away by you, I'll forget him. Well, I don't. I can't. I never will. I don't even think he loves me, if you want to know the truth. But even if he doesn't, I still love him.'

'You're disgusting.' Paul looked deeply offended, and I was suddenly afraid I had gone too far and really hurt his feelings. His wiring was extremely sensitive, and I knew how easy it was to bruise his ego. 'And you're right. He doesn't love you. I don't think he knows how. That's why he built me. He wanted me to do all the fancy footwork. And I do. Let's face it, Steph. I make him look good. Without me, he's nothing.'

'Without him, you are,' I said bluntly, and Paul looked as though I'd hit him. I wanted to stop then, but I couldn't. I knew that for the sake of my own sanity, I had to be honest with him. I was crazy about him. I enjoyed him endlessly. I had never had as much fun before, and I cared about him deeply, but in the past two days I had discovered what I had always suspected secretly. I didn't love him. I loved Peter. Utterly, completely, and truly. Even if Peter never understood it. That still didn't change it.

'You hurt my feelings, Steph,' Paul said, pulling the vodka bottle out again, and taking a long swig from the bottle. And then he burped loudly as he set it back down on the table. It was one of those little things I loved about him.

'I'm sorry, Paul. I had to say it.'

'I don't believe you. And neither does Peter. He knows you love me.'

'What makes you think so?'

'He told me,' Paul said bravely. 'He called before he left for San Francisco.'

'What did he say?' I asked, curious about the things they talked about, and what they said about me. Contemplating that was more than a little unnerving. No woman liked to think of both her lovers conferring.

'He just said you'd been depressed ever since he got back, and he needed to get away. He's been getting much too close to you, apparently.

He missed you a lot when he was away. And he said he could see when he returned how much you missed me. You did, didn't you?' He grinned victoriously at me.

'I always miss you,' I said honestly. 'And I was depressed thinking I might not see you again.'

'Why wouldn't you?' The Klone looked puzzled.

'I wouldn't see you if I left him, Paul. We talked about it.'

'Why would you leave him, if you supposedly love him so much?'

'Because he doesn't love me. And I can't play this game forever, sleeping with both of you. It's not decent, and it's too tough an adjustment. One minute I'm bounding off the walls with you, and trying to keep you from mooning the buses on Fifth Avenue, the next I'm trying to be respectable with him, and adjust to what his needs are. And whatever they are, I'm not sure that they include me at the moment. He barely said good-bye to me when he left for California.'

'Because he knows that we belong together.'

'You belong in the shop, with your head off. And I belong in the nuthouse.' But much more to the point, I knew I belonged with Peter. Forever, if he'd let me. But that seemed unlikely now.

'He doesn't want to stand between us,' Paul said with confidence, as though he knew Peter better than I did, and spoke for him.

'Then he's crazier than you are.' But before I could say more, the children came home from their weekend with Roger and Helena, and wanted to complain about it. They were used to Paul by then, and the exotic outfits he wore, that they scarcely noticed him sitting in the kitchen, and of course they thought it was Peter.

'Nice pants,' Charlotte commented as she helped herself to a Dr Pepper and continued to complain about what a bitch Helena was, and how disgusting she looked with her boobs bigger than ever, while I urged her to be respectful. It was useless. I was still talking to her when Paul disappeared with Sam conspiratorially, and I almost had a heart attack half an hour later, when I went to look for them, and saw Paul hand him a live iguana. He had it in his suitcase.

'Oh my *God*!' I screamed. 'What *is* that?'

'His name is Iggy,' Sam said proudly. 'A friend of Peter's brought him back from Venezuela.'

'Well, tell him to take it back there. You can't have that thing in this house, Sam.' I was panicked.

'Oh, Mom . . .' Sam turned his huge eyes up to mine and begged me.

'No! *Never!*' And then I turned to Paul in fury. Not only had he come uninvited as usual, and unwanted this time, but he had brought a monster with him. 'You can make a lovely pair of boots out of him, one at least. I'm sure your friend in Venezuela can find you another. You won't even have to dye them. They're green already. Now put that thing back in your suitcase!' Paul picked him up off Sam's head, where he had been resting, and cradled him lovingly, while Sam continued to beg me to keep him. 'Forget it, both of you! Get rid of him. Or I'm sending both of you to Venezuela with him. Good-bye, Iggy!' I said pointedly and went back to the kitchen to cook dinner. What was I going to do with him? And with or without Iggy, this time I knew Paul was not going to be staying. I had made a decision.

I was cooking pasta when Paul walked back into the kitchen again, with a serious expression. 'I'm disappointed in you, Steph. You've lost your sense of humor.'

'I've grown up. You wouldn't understand. You're not real. You can afford to be Peter Pan forever. I can't. I'm a grown woman, with two children.'

'You sound like Peter. He always says stuff like that. That's why everyone thinks he's so boring.'

'Maybe that's why I love him. Besides, he would never do a thing like that, bring something like that to Sam. A goldfish maybe, or a hamster. Maybe a dog. But not a helio-monster or whatever that thing is.'

'He's an iguana, and he's a beauty. And what makes you think he wouldn't do that? You don't know him.'

'I know him intimately, and believe me, he would *not* give my son an iguana.'

'Well, pardon me for living,' he said, pulling out the cooking sherry and drinking half the bottle. 'Do I have time for a shower before dinner?'

'No,' I said firmly, 'and you can't stay here tonight.'

'Why not?' He looked disappointed as he started to hiccup. 'That sherry is awful, by the way, you shouldn't use it.'

'You shouldn't drink it.'

'I finished the vodka, and you're out of bourbon.'

'I didn't know you were coming. Peter only drinks martinis.'

'I don't care what he drinks. And why can't I stay here?'

'Because I'm turning over a new leaf. I think he was really upset about you this time. I don't want to screw up a relationship that's important to me, even if he did send you.'

'Isn't it a little late for that? Besides, you don't even think he loves you.' He sounded mean when he said it. It was the vodka talking. Or maybe the sherry.

'That's not the point. Whether he loves me

or not, I love him. And you can't sleep here.'

'I can't go back to the shop,' he said stubbornly. 'I don't have the keys, and it's closed on Sundays.'

'Then stay at the Plaza. You have his American Express card. Charge it to Peter.'

'Only if you stay there with me.'

'Forget it . . . and besides, I don't have a sitter,' I said, distracted, as the pasta started burning. All the water had boiled off while we discussed the iguana and whether or not he could sleep there.

'Then I'll stay here,' he said practically. 'Till he comes back from California.'

'Paul,' I said firmly, looking him squarely in the eyes, 'you can stay for dinner, but after that, you're leaving.' And I wasn't kidding, as Charlotte walked into the room and looked at both of us with a curious expression.

'Who's Paul?' she asked, wondering what game we were playing. 'What happened to dinner?'

'I burned it,' I said through clenched teeth, glaring at both of them, as Sam wandered in, holding the iguana.

'Get that thing out of here!' I screamed at him, as I dropped the pot of burned pasta in the sink. It was beyond salvation.

'I hate you!' Sam said, as he went back to his room with Iggy.

'You really should let him keep it,' Paul said gently, 'it means a lot to him.'

'Get out of my life!' I said, wanting to scream or cry or hit him.

'You won't let me,' he said, smiling at Charlotte. 'Your mother gets very nervous when she cooks, doesn't she? Do you want me to whip something up?' he offered helpfully, as I pulled a frozen pizza out of the freezer.

'No, thank you.' He took out the liar's dice then, and started playing with Charlotte, as I banged and slammed my way around the kitchen.

It was nine o'clock by the time I served dinner, and I somehow managed to burn the pizza.

It was after ten when I finished cleaning up the kitchen. Sam was asleep in his room by then, and he still had the iguana with him. When I went to kiss him good night, I saw it lying next to him, on the pillow, and closed the door gently so it couldn't escape. Paul was going to have to take it with him. I was never going to let Sam keep it.

'Is he asleep?' Paul asked gently, as I came back to the kitchen. He was working on my only bottle of sapphire gin. I had been saving it for Peter, but it didn't seem to matter as much suddenly. Peter had said we 'had to talk,' which was always a death knell. He was probably going to dump me when he came back from California, if he hadn't already. He probably just hadn't had the guts to tell me. I remembered how quiet he had been when we walked in the park in the snow, and the way he had looked at me after he saw the ruby ring Paul gave me.

I poured myself a small glass of the gin, poured some tonic in it, and threw in a couple of ice cubes.

'I thought you didn't drink.' He looked shocked when he saw it.

'I don't. But I think I need it.'

'How about a massage?'

'How about taking your iguana and going to

a hotel, without me?' I had had all I could take for one night, two burned dinners, a romance on the rocks, and a giant lizard loose in my son's bedroom, not to mention this lunatic I'd been sleeping with, who had probably cost me my relationship with Peter. And Paul wasn't even human. My life was a shambles. I'd been shaving my legs religiously for two years, had sworn off blueberries, had met the finest man I'd ever known, and managed to screw it up somehow by having an affair with R2D2.

'I think you should go to see Dr Steinfeld,' Paul said sympathetically as he watched me sipping my gin and tonic.

'Maybe we all should.' I was too tired to pursue the subject further. All I wanted was to see Peter, instead of Paul, sitting comfortably in my kitchen in his scarlet leggings. 'Don't those things itch? I can't wear them.' I was slowly getting drunk on one drink and didn't care. My life was over anyway. I had lost Peter.

'Yes, they do,' Paul said conversationally, indifferent to the desperation I was feeling. 'I'll take them off in a minute.'

'Not here,' I said pointedly, and he smiled.

'Of course not. I meant in the bedroom.' I sat back in the kitchen chair, and groaned, with my eyes closed. Why had Peter done this to me? Why couldn't he have picked up someone else in Paris and inflicted his Klone on some other unsuspecting woman? I was in love with Jekyll and Hyde. Jekyll mostly, and he didn't want me. And I couldn't get Hyde the hell out of my life, my hair, or my kitchen. And I was exhausted from trying. 'Where's Charlotte?' he asked with mild concern as he got up and stretched.

'Asleep.' She had gone to bed right after Sam had.

'So early?'

'I asked her to clean up her room and do her homework. That's like giving her nitrous oxide. She passed out as soon as I said it.' It also explained why the apartment was so peaceful.

I finished the gin and tonic and stood up, looking at him, wondering if there was any hope of getting rid of him that night, but I didn't think so. It might just be easier to let him sleep there, one last time, and then throw him and his iguana out in the morning.

'Why don't you sleep in the guest room?' I suggested, giving in, but not completely. He could have my guest room, but not my virtue, or my heart. They belonged to Peter. I was sure now. I was not going to be swayed again, into believing that I loved Paul. I didn't. And then I remembered. The guest room was full of Christmas presents, and it would have taken hours to remove them. I had been piling them up in there for days, and I had nowhere else to put them. They weren't wrapped yet, and I didn't want the kids to see them. You couldn't even find the bed in there. The situation was distressing. 'I just remembered. You can't sleep there. You can sleep on the floor of my bedroom.'

'I can't,' he said convincingly, as my whole body sagged listening to him. I was losing the man I loved, and couldn't get rid of the Klone he had inflicted on me. 'I can't sleep on the floor,' he explained, 'it's bad for my wiring. It distorts it.'

'I'll call an electrician for you tomorrow. That's your only option.'

'You're all heart, Steph.'

'Thank you.' I turned off the lights, put my glass in the sink, and he followed me to my bedroom. And as soon as I closed the door, he stripped off the red spandex leggings. I tried not to see how great his legs were. Having been made with great precision and great care, his legs were every bit as splendid as Peter's.

I disappeared into the bathroom and put on a nightgown and a robe, and tied it. I would have slept in my ski clothes if I could have. I was determined to resist him.

'Are you cold?' he asked, looking surprised by the bathrobe.

'No, frigid,' I said simply, and climbed into bed, as he went to brush his teeth. He was good about those things, even though he had no need to go to the dentist. His teeth were white and perfect, and were actually made of porcelain over some very rare metal. He had explained it to me once when I asked him. He had no idea what it was to get a filling. Lucky devil.

And when he returned from the bathroom, the lights were off and I pretended to be sleeping. I was lying on my side at the edge of the bed, and I fully expected him to sleep on the floor, which was another sign of insanity on my part. He had no intention of it. And within seconds, I felt him slip into bed beside me. I couldn't see if he was wearing Peter's pajamas, but prayed he was. And then I heard him strike a match, and knew what he was doing. He was lighting the candle, but I didn't dare say anything for fear he would know I wasn't sleeping, and then a moment later, I felt him gently touch my shoulders and start to massage them. I lay there, tense, hating him for being so nice to me. But I knew there was a reason for it. I knew exactly what he wanted, and I was determined that, for once, no matter how enticing he was, he wouldn't get it.

But I had to admit as he massaged my shoulders, and rubbed my back, it was incredibly relaxing. And after a while, in spite of myself, I sighed, and rolled over on my stomach.

'Better?' he whispered in the candlelight, and the sound of his voice always made me feel sensual and happy, and tonight it made me feel just a little sad. He sounded just like Peter.

He moved closer to me to massage my arms, and intent on resisting him, I stiffened. 'Don't come any closer. I have a loaded gun in the pocket of my nightgown.'

'So shoot me.'

'It'll screw up your wiring forever.'

'I think you're worth it.' But this time, even though I loved the sound and feel of him, I wasn't swayed. I wasn't hooked. I wasn't swooning. All I could think about was Peter. 'What are you thinking?' he asked as he worked his way down my back again, and then massaged my buttocks.

'I was thinking about him,' I admitted sleepily, my voice funny from the pressure of his hands on my back. 'I miss him. Do you suppose he'll come back . . . to me, I mean? . . . I think he hates me.'

'No, he doesn't,' he said softly. 'I think he loves you.'

'Are you serious?' I asked, rolling over on my back to look at him. It was the nicest thing he'd said all night, and then I realized it was a ruse to make me look at him, as he leaned over and kissed me. 'Don't . . .' I whispered in the candlelight, but the word was lost as he continued to kiss me. I didn't forget Peter then, only myself, as his hands began to move slowly beneath my nightgown. 'Paul . . . don't . . . I can't . . .'

'Just one last time . . . please . . . and then I swear I won't come back again . . .' But this time, when he said it, I knew I wouldn't miss him. Our time was over.

'We shouldn't . . .' I tried valiantly to resist him, and then wondered what difference it would make. Just one last time . . . for old times' sake . . . something to remember. And before I could stop him, he had started making love to me, and my dressing gown and nightgown disappeared somewhere onto the floor, as I abandoned myself to him, knowing full well I shouldn't. But it was hard to remember anything as my body sang at his touch. It was a song I knew I would long remember. It would be something to dream of, after both Peter and Paul left me. Just one more memory of a time of madness.

And as I gave in to him completely, he held me in his arms and I could feel him preparing to soar into the air and do one last quadruple

flip with me. I smiled as I felt it begin, too transported by him to resist it. It felt as though we
were suspended in midair forever, and as we
prepared to land gracefully, as we always did,
I felt him move only slightly differently, but just
enough to change both our velocity and our
direction, and before I knew what had
happened to me, we had bounced off the bed,
hit a chair, and crashed into a table, with arms
and legs everywhere, a foot suddenly near my
ear, and as we fell like a meteorite falling to
earth, I heard a crash and saw his head at an
appalling angle. I wondered, as we lay there,
gasping for air, if I was finally going to see him
with his head off.

I tried to sit up, but he was lying on top of
me, and I couldn't. 'Oh shit, what happened?'
I could hardly get the words out, and wondered
if all my ribs were broken. 'Are you okay?' It
was a useless question. The chair was on top of
us as well, and he looked as though he were
eating my nightgown. The sound of whatever
it was he was saying to me was muffled. I pulled
the nightgown off his face, and realized he was

going to get a black eye from the chair leg. 'What did you say?'

'I said, are you okay?'

'I'm not sure yet.' He grinned sheepishly at me, and propped himself up, wincing, on one elbow. 'I think I moved wrong.'

'Maybe I did.' It wasn't like him to miss it. 'Would ice help?' I actually felt sorry for him, as much as his wires, I suspect he had bruised his ego. He was definitely not as agile as he had been. Maybe it was the vodka. He was used to bourbon.

I went to get him some ice, and a snifter of brandy. I knew that sometimes he liked that. And there was no Yquem left. He took a sip of the brandy, and I put the ice gingerly on his neck and shoulder. It made him seem almost human.

'Steph . . .' He was looking at me strangely as I ministered to him, and I propped him up on pillows. He looked so sweet and vulnerable, and I suddenly panicked, wondering what Peter would say if I broke him.

'It's a hell of a note to end on, isn't it?' Maybe

it was a sign that it was truly over between us.

'We'll have to try again sometime,' he said, looking at me, a little glazed from the brandy.

'I don't think so,' I said sadly.

'Why not?' He was so damn persistent, it must have been something in his computer.

'You know why.'

'Because of him.' I nodded, there was no need to say it all again. I had already said it. Before he tried to kill me with his failed quadruple. 'He's not worth it.'

'I think he is.' That I was sure of.

'He doesn't deserve you.' He looked wistful as he said it.

'Neither do you.' I smiled at him. 'You need a nice Klone like you, with a strong back, and a better computer.'

'Did I hurt you, Steph?'

'I'm okay.' It was going to be an odd life now without him, and I already felt nostalgic thinking about it. In spite of myself, I knew I would miss him. Who else would wear red spandex and lime green satin, not to mention the leopard G-string? There would never again be anyone else like him. Not even Peter. But even as I lay beside the naked splendor of his Klone, all I could think about was Peter.

'Why do you love him?'

'I just do. It feels right.'

'Does it?' He was watching me, as he handed me the brandy snifter, and I sipped it. It seared my throat as I took a tiny swallow. 'It feels right to me too,' he said then in a whisper.

'Don't start that again,' I warned him, as I noticed that his eye was bruising. He was going to have a terrific shiner to show for the quadruple.

'Steph . . .' he said again. 'I have a confession to make.'

'What now?' By then, nothing would have surprised me.

'I never called him.'

'Who? Peter? Were you supposed to?' He hadn't called me either. He was probably in the arms of Helena's twin in San Francisco.

'No, Paul.'

'Paul who?' I was tired, and his confession didn't sound too intriguing. The brandy must have been getting to him.

'He's still in the shop, with his head off.'

'Who is?' And then slowly, as I looked at him, the full force of what he was saying began to hit me. But it couldn't be. It wasn't possible. He would never do this. 'What are you saying to me?'

'You know what I'm saying . . . I'm not him . . . I'm me . . .' He looked like a little boy as he said it.

'Peter?' I said hoarsely, as though seeing him for the first time, and then I understood the crash in the midst of the quadruple flip. It wasn't Paul lying in bed with me at all. It was Peter. And I was stunned as I knew it. 'Peter! You didn't . . . you couldn't . . . why would you?' I pulled away to look at him, but there was no way to tell them apart now, except for the bruises.

'I thought you were in love with Paul when I came back this time. I wanted to know for sure. I missed you so much when I was in California . . . it was all I could think of, and then I came back and you looked so sad. I thought you were in love with him, and didn't want to see me.'

'I thought you didn't love me.' I was still appalled by what he had just done, and nearly angry, but he was so banged up, it was hard to be as angry as I should have. 'You seemed so cold . . . so distant . . .'

'I do love you. I just thought it was Paul you wanted to be with. I thought he was what you wanted.'

'So did I, once or twice,' I grinned at him sheepishly, 'but I finally figured it out. He's not real to me . . . you are. You're much more wonderful than he is.' In spite of myself, I leaned over and kissed him, and he winced when I touched him, but he kissed me, and when he did, I knew the answer to all my questions.

'I can't do the quadruple,' Peter said regretfully, 'or drink the way he does. I don't know how they programmed him. I'm going to have a hell of a hangover tomorrow.'

'You deserve it,' I said, snuggling next to him, and pulling the covers up around us. He was shivering a little. It had been quite an evening.

'There are a lot of things I can't do like him,' Peter said, with an arm around me.

'Most things you do a lot better. I'm too old for all the acrobatics.'

'I'm too old to lose you, Steph. I love you. I don't want to lose this.' It was everything I had wanted Roger to say a thousand years before, and he hadn't. Peter was the one I had waited a lifetime for. Even if he was a little crazy.

'Where is Paul now?' I asked, curious suddenly. It was hard to believe he hadn't been with me all night . . . the clothes . . . the things he had said . . . the iguana . . . Peter had been terrifyingly convincing.

'He's in the shop, and he's going to stay there. With his head off. After Christmas, you're coming to California with me. From now on, when I travel, we'll get a sitter for the kids and you'll come with me.' He pulled me just a little closer, as I snuggled beside him, unable to believe what I was hearing. This was the dream. Everything that had come before it had been the nightmare.

'Why didn't we think of that from the beginning?'

'I thought you'd have more fun with him, and you wouldn't want to leave the kids, so I activated him for you. I thought you'd like him.'

'I did. But it just got too crazy. I'd rather get a sitter, and go with you.'

'The kids won't mind too much if you leave them?'

'They're old enough to manage without me from time to time.' And then I thought of something that worried me considerably, as I looked up at Peter. 'What about the iguana?'

'Consider it a last gift from Paul.'

'Do I have to?' This was not the best news of the evening, but I didn't want to hurt his feelings, or break Sam's heart. I just didn't want to have to see the beast at breakfast, staring into my cornflakes. Maybe we could make a cage for him, or rent him his own apartment.

'You'll grow to love him,' Peter promised, blowing out the candle, and pulling me closer again as we cuddled under the covers.

'The last time you said that, you turned my life into a shambles. Or Paul did.' Just looking back at his exploits now seemed beyond belief as Peter held me.

'I plan to do that myself from now on . . . turn your life into a shambles. Maybe I should keep the gold lamé disco pants as a souvenir,' he said

301

softly, drifting off to sleep as I looked at him, wondering how all this had happened. I knew I would never completely understand it. I couldn't help wondering if it was all a figment of my imagination. It was hard to believe it had happened. 'I love you Steph . . . I'm here now,' he whispered, and indeed he was, as he fell asleep in my arms, and I drifted off beside him. He was there, as I was. And I was his now. It all seemed so simple in the end. I thought of Paul for a millisecond as I fell asleep, and I knew that, in spite of everything, I wouldn't miss him. It was over. We didn't need him anymore. We had each other. Forever. The two of us from now on, and no more Klone. Just Peter and I.

THE END

THE LONG ROAD HOME
by Danielle Steel

A harrowing journey into the dark side of childhood.

From her secret perch at the top of the stairs, seven-year-old Gabriella watches the guests arrive at her parents' lavish Manhattan home. The click, click, click of her mother's high heels strikes terror into her heart. Her world is a confusing blend of terror, betrayal and pain, and she knows that there is no safe place for her to hide.

When her parents' marriage collapses, her mother abandons her to a convent, where Gabriella's battered body and soul begin to mend amid the quiet safety and hushed rituals of the nuns. And when she grows into womanhood, young Father Joe Connors comes into her life. Like Gabriella, Joe is haunted by the pain of his childhood, and with her he takes the first steps towards healing. But their relationship leads to disaster as Joe must choose between the priesthood and Gabriella. She struggles to survive on her own in New York, where she seeks escape through her writing, until eventually she is able to find forgiveness, freedom from guilt, and healing.

In this work of daring and compassion, Danielle Steel has created a vivid portrait of an abused child's broken world which will shock and move you to your very soul.

0 552 14502 5

A LIST OF OTHER DANIELLE STEEL TITLES AVAILABLE FROM CORGI BOOKS AND BANTAM PRESS

THE PRICES SHOWN BELOW WERE CORRECT AT THE TIME OF GOING TO PRESS. HOWEVER TRANSWORLD PUBLISHERS RESERVE THE RIGHT TO SHOW NEW RETAIL PRICES ON COVERS WHICH MAY DIFFER FROM THOSE PREVIOUSLY ADVERTISED IN THE TEXT OR ELSEWHERE.

13523 2	NO GREATER LOVE	£5.99
13525 9	HEARTBEAT	£5.99
13522 4	DADDY	£5.99
13524 0	MESSAGE FROM NAM	£5.99
13745 6	JEWELS	£5.99
13746 4	MIXED BLESSINGS	£5.99
13526 7	VANISHED	£5.99
13747 2	ACCIDENT	£5.99
14245 X	THE GIFT	£5.99
13748 0	WINGS	£5.99
13749 9	LIGHTNING	£5.99
14378 2	FIVE DAYS IN PARIS	£5.99
14131 3	MALICE	£5.99
14132 1	SILENT HONOUR	£5.99
14133 X	THE RANCH	£5.99
14507 6	SPECIAL DELIVERY	£5.99
14504 1	THE GHOST	£5.99
14502 5	THE LONG ROAD HOME	£5.99
04075 9	GRANNY DAN (Hardback)	£9.99
03439 2	MIRROR IMAGE (Hardback)	£16.99
04487 8	HIS BRIGHT LIGHT (Hardback)	£16.99
04070 8	BITTERSWEET (Hardback)	£16.99

Transworld titles are available by post from:

Book Service By Post, PO Box 29, Douglas, Isle of Man, IM99 1BQ

Credit cards accepted. Please telephone 01624 675137
fax 01624 670923, Internet http://www.bookpost.co.uk
or e-mail: bookshop@enterprise.net for details

Free postage and packing in the UK. Overseas customers: allow £1 per book (paperbacks) and £3 per book (hardbacks).